"I can protect you. I can give you security. I can give you the world."

"But not your love." She no longer seemed to feel anything—not the room's cold air, not the fire in her stomach, not the feelings that should be ripping through her like a tornado.

"There are more solid things between a man and a woman than useless feelings."

"Like what?" Could Daniel have forgotten the passion they'd once shared?

"Like the things you say you want, Christiane. Family, roots, security."

Her voice could not climb up her throat. A tiny sound echoed inside her like a wounded cry. She checked her cheeks with a quick flick of her hand to make sure no moisture stained them, betraying the ease with which he could tear open old wounds.

"Trust me." He said the words so softly, she had to strain to catch them. Their gazes met and held. His weighty sadness mixed with hers and wove a bond of regret for all that might have been, all that could never be.

"The last time I trusted you," she blurted out, "I ended up pregnant."

Dear Harlequin Intrigue Reader,

As we ring in a new year, we have another great month of mystery and suspense coupled with steamy passion.

Here are some juicy highlights from our six-book lineup:

- Julie Miller launches a new series, THE PRECINCT, beginning with *Partner-Protector*. These books revolve around the rugged Fourth Precinct lawmen of Kansas City whom you first fell in love with in the TAYLOR CLAN series!

- *Rocky Mountain Mystery* marks the beginning of Cassie Miles's riveting new trilogy, COLORADO CRIME CONSULTANTS, about a network of private citizens who volunteer their expertise in solving criminal investigations.

- Those popular TOP SECRET BABIES return to our lineup for the next *four* months!

- Gothic-inspired tales continue in our spine-tingling ECLIPSE promotion.

And don't forget to look for Debra Webb's special Signature Spotlight title this month: *Dying To Play*.

Hopefully we've whetted your appetite for January's thrilling lineup. And be sure to check back every month to satisfy your craving for outstanding suspense reading.

Enjoy!

Denise O'Sullivan
Senior Editor
Harlequin Intrigue

A ROSE
AT MIDNIGHT

SYLVIE KURTZ

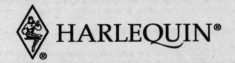

TORONTO • NEW YORK • LONDON
AMSTERDAM • PARIS • SYDNEY • HAMBURG
STOCKHOLM • ATHENS • TOKYO • MILAN • MADRID
PRAGUE • WARSAW • BUDAPEST • AUCKLAND

Pour Maman et Papa—avec amour.
and
For Linda Kruger and Denise O'Sullivan—with appreciation.

Author's Note

Some of the dates, location and order of events of the Carnaval were
altered to suit story purposes. The tale of Rose Latulippe is one I
remember from my childhood—the most vivid version being the one
from a children's program called *Franfreluche*.

ISBN 0-373-22822-8

A ROSE AT MIDNIGHT

Copyright © 2005 by Sylvie Kurtz

ABOUT THE AUTHOR

Flying an eight-hour solo cross-country in a Piper Arrow with only the airplane's crackling radio and a large bag of M&M's for company, Sylvie Kurtz realized a pilot's life wasn't for her. The stories zooming in and out of her mind proved more entertaining than the flight itself. Not a quitter, she finished her pilot's course and earned her commercial license and instrument rating.

Since then, she has traded in her wings for a keyboard where she lets her imagination soar to create fictional adventures that explore the power of love and the thrill of suspense. When not writing, she enjoys the outdoors with her husband and two children, quilt-making, photography and reading whatever catches her interest.

You can write to Sylvie at
P.O. Box 702, Milford, NH 03055.
And visit her Web site at www.sylviekurtz.com.

Books by Sylvie Kurtz

CAST OF CHARACTERS

Christiane Lawrence—She's seeking roots in her history. She's finding a whole lot more.

Daniel Moreau—He can speak with his music—words come much harder.

Rosane Lawrence—She's the daughter Daniel tried to protect.

Armand Langelier—His obsession brought them all together.

Marguerite Langelier—The years have etched resentment on her face.

Caroline Lawrence—She's the one mistake Armand has allowed himself.

Francine Beaulieu—She's the curious next-door neighbor.

Jean-Paul Dubuc—He's Daniel's bulldog manager. He shaped Daniel's career, and he won't let Daniel lose his star status over a woman.

Chapter One

Feelings were for fools and Daniel Moreau hadn't played the fool for anyone in years.

But he felt her presence before he turned around. Felt her in a way that grated against the ruthless control he'd cultivated since that night nine years ago when his world had turned upside down. Felt her and knew with certainty that her presence here was no accident of fate.

Did she know she was being used? Probably not. Christiane Lawrence was too trusting for her own good. That more than anything made her a threat to him.

He watched with predatory curiosity as the white-gloved butler took her snow-colored coat. Watched as red-jacketed waiters offered her tantalizing tidbits and generous goblets of wine from silver platters. Watched as Armand Langelier took her elbow and guided her to their hostess, Madame Bernier. And found an unexpected possessiveness grounding itself somewhere between his boots and his brain.

With a shake of his head, Daniel dismissed the errant feeling. She wasn't his anymore.

Her dangling blue and silver icicle earrings were

an anomaly in a sea of diamonds and sapphires. He guessed she'd worn them as a conversation starter. For all the quiet sophistication of her clothes and careful style of her short blond hair, he remembered her as shy. She moved with confidence, the soft silk and the flattering cut of her dove-gray cocktail dress shifting pleasantly with each of her steps. Subdued class— one of the many things he'd liked about Christiane.

Armand leaned down to whisper something in her ear, and she laughed in response. Though he could not hear the sound, it rippled through him. Her laughter. Her voice. They'd once cracked open a lock he'd thought rusted shut. Daniel's fists tightened by his side. Not this time.

The older man's gaze shifted to the crowd. Looking for him, no doubt. What was the point of making such a bold move if Armand couldn't witness the expected reaction?

Daniel had worked hard to hide his secrets, to bury his past, to make amends. And now it could all change. Just like that. All because of this woman.

Funny how the world kept going as if nothing was wrong. People still laughed. The quartet still played. Sequined dresses still sparkled in the light on this cold February night. He'd expected the crack of thunder, the flare of lightning, the crash of a storm, some sort of force of nature to herald his doom.

But it came quietly—just when he'd started to think everything in his life had at last fallen into place.

''There you are.'' Jean-Paul Dubuc, his manager, clasped an overeager hand around Daniel's shoulder. He reminded Daniel of a bulldog—short, squat, bald and ugly, but fiercely loyal. A good man to have on your side. Except tonight. He'd ask too many questions, and Daniel would have too few answers.

"I've been looking all over for you." Jean-Paul tried to shepherd him toward the ballroom where the piano stood waiting. "Time to get the show on the road."

"Not now." Daniel shrugged off Jean-Paul's hold and searched the crowd for Christiane. The silver of her earrings winked in the distance.

"Daniel," Jean-Paul insisted. "Madame Bernier is waiting."

"Not now."

"It's you they came to hear, not some nameless quartet."

"Then they'll wait." Daniel had to warn her. It was the least he could do.

"What's wrong with you?" His manager frowned and looked him over for signs of disease or disaster—the latter probably being the more worrisome of the two for a scrapper like Jean-Paul.

"See that woman over there?" Daniel thrust his chin in Christiane's direction. Armand gave her a little bow and headed for the bar.

"The one in the gray dress?"

Daniel nodded. "She'll destroy me."

He'd said it for shock value, and Jean-Paul didn't disappoint him. "Who is she?" The creases above Jean-Paul's eyes deepened. His jowls quivered. "What did you do? What's she holding over you?"

A humorless grin tugged at the corners of Daniel's mouth. He was sick of the whole business, of being handled, of never-ending expectations. He was sick of it all. "Worried about damage control?"

"Do I need to be?"

Daniel's gaze raked the crowd until he found Christiane again, introducing herself to two women with overteased hair. "Not if I play the game right."

"Non, mais t'as finalement perdu la boule! You've gone completely mad." Jean-Paul stomped in a half-moon around Daniel as if his leash was too short. "It's not exactly the time to go over the edge, Daniel."

"I'm still in control. I know the rules this time."

"This time?" Jean-Paul stopped short and stared at his client. "What are you talking about?"

"Strategy."

"Now listen, Daniel." Jean-Paul shook his finger at the middle of Daniel's chest. "I'm depending on you. Madame Bernier is depending on you. All those people who paid a small fortune for a ticket to hear you play your new piece next week are depending on you. I need to know I didn't waste my time promoting you to stardom just to have you crash when we've finally made it."

Jean-Paul stopped waving his finger and planted it on Daniel's chest. "You owe me. Where would you be today if it weren't for me?"

Without looking at the annoying digit, Daniel swiped away Jean-Paul's finger. "Right here."

"Maybe." Jean-Paul shrugged. "More likely you'd be sitting in a jail somewhere for banging your fists on somebody's face instead of a keyboard."

"Have I ever let you down?"

Jean-Paul shuffled his feet. "Not yet."

"Not ever." Daniel loosed a short, sharp laugh and swept one arm to encompass the glaringly bright room. "Why would I want to risk giving all this up?"

Jean-Paul's jaw moved in a slow contemplative circle. "Music *is* your life."

"My soul," Daniel said mockingly as he watched Christiane work her way around the room as if she'd done this a thousand times.

Jean-Paul panted with worry. "So what are you going to do about this girl?"

As Daniel considered his options, the party kept up its bright pace around him. "Have you ever had to make a choice between two impossibles?"

"Every day when I try to plan your schedule."

"I meant important things."

Jean-Paul frowned. "What's more important than molding your career?"

"Life or breath."

"They're the same."

"Exactly."

"Now I know you're going crazy." Jean-Paul shook his head slowly, causing the light to dance on his balding pate. "Promise me you won't blow your image of the dashing, tall, dark and handsome hero until *after* you've fulfilled your contract's obligations."

"Worried about your commission?"

Jean-Paul's jaw dropped. "That's not fair, and you know it. About the girl…"

If Christiane was in Quebec City, it could only mean one thing. Armand was going to try to use her just as he'd tried to use her mother.

"I'll do the only thing I can," Daniel said, resigned. He'd once found heaven and had to put her through hell. Now she was in danger. He had to protect her. And there was only one way she'd allow him that close.

"Which is?"

"Marry her."

HER PRESENCE here seemed fated, Christi reflected. A month ago if anyone had told her she'd be in Quebec City discovering roots she'd never known she had, she would have told them they were nuts. Yet here she was, three thousand miles from home, accompanying her mother's cousin to a party launching two weeks of winter carnival celebrations—and feeling more at home than she'd ever dreamed.

This vacation was exactly what she'd needed after dealing with the trauma of her parents' accidental deaths a few months ago. In Armand's home, her mother's presence wrapped around her like childhood comfort, and it eased the pain of her loss.

For the past few days, Armand and his sister, Marguerite, had proved gracious hosts. Marguerite had spoiled Christi and her daughter Rosane, with home-cooked meals. Armand had entertained them with stories from his youth. As he talked about her mother with love and told her of his memories of their shared childhood, Christi had relaxed. Her belligerent stomach, on fire since her parents' accident, seemed to have taken a recess, too. She hadn't had to unpack the half-dozen rolls of Tums at the bottom of her suitcase or use the emergency one tucked in her purse. Even her dour daughter's demeanor had softened. Rosane had actually smiled at some of Armand's outrageous sleight-of-hand tricks.

"It was very kind of you to include me this evening," Christi said to Armand after their hostess fluttered away.

"Nonsense, as one of the directors of the arts committee, it is my prerogative to invite whomever I desire." His thick French accent was unmistakable despite his flawless English. His impeccable tux, neatly groomed black mustache and slicked-back charcoal hair reminded her of the perfect gentlemen in old black-and-white movies. His slow, gracious charm put her at ease here as it had since she'd arrived in Quebec City.

"Besides," he continued, "I needed an escort, and with you on my arm, I am the envy of every man here."

She laughed. "You're quite the flatterer, aren't you?"

"One of my many charms." His white teeth shone and his dark eyes glittered with good humor. "Can I get you anything, *ma chère?*"

"Some sparkling water, please." She didn't want to chance alcohol now that her stomach was finally behaving.

"I shall return momentarily." Armand bowed and moved in the direction of the bar at the other end of the cavernous room.

When Armand had invited her to a party at a friend's home, she'd expected a quaint little house, not a mansion. And this mansion fell just short of a palace as far as she was concerned. Antique furniture was arranged in cozy sets for easy conversation. Large portions of the marble floor lay bare for those who preferred to mingle or dance. Fresh greenery adorned with carnival masks and opalescent streamers decorated everything from priceless paintings to the curving cherrywood staircase ascending to the second floor. Multicolored lights and flickering candles in sconces gave the whole place a festive atmosphere.

As she mingled her way around the room, she caught snatches of conversation.

"He's simply marvelous," an older lady said, fanning her face with a hand.

"Can you believe his show next week sold out in less than one hour?" said another. "I waited in line all day for the ticket window to open for nothing!"

"Every time I hear him play, I fall in love."

"Speaking of love, I heard he met someone. In France. Or was it England? There's talk of wedding bells."

"Pity."

"Not for her. Not with the contract he just signed."

Christi introduced herself to several people, passed a group of gray-haired, tuxedoed men and was about to join a group of women who seemed about her age when a commotion at the archway between this room and the next caught her attention.

Madame Bernier stood on a chair and clapped her hands. In her green and gold sequined dress, she looked like an overweight hummingbird. "Attention everyone," she said in French. "Let's all make our way to the ballroom. The music is about to start."

Like salmon spawning, everyone hurried in the direction of the ballroom, murmuring excitedly as they went. Christi lagged behind.

"Can I have everyone's attention?" Madame Bernier waited a few minutes for the chatter to die down and the last person to squeeze into the ballroom.

Christi found a spot at the back of the room, but couldn't see the musician everyone seemed to have gone gaga over.

"As you all know this simple gala is to welcome home our favorite pianist," Madame Bernier said.

"He's just finished a smashing European tour. Next week, as part of the Mardi Gras Masked Ball, he will perform a piece commissioned by the arts committee especially for the event. I'm told it's called 'A Rose at Midnight.'" The crowd oohed their approval. "He's graciously offered to donate all the proceeds to the young artist grant program sponsored by the arts committee." Madame Bernier raised her hands and clapped, encouraging the crowd to do likewise. The response was almost deafening.

When the roar died down, Madame Bernier spoke again. "Tonight, as a special favor to me, he's agreed to treat us to a sample of his best-known pieces." With one hand, she waved grandly at the piano. "Everyone help me welcome home Daniel Moreau!"

Daniel Moreau.

The name echoed and reechoed inside the chamber of her brain.

The crowd clapped. Each meeting of palm against palm cracked like shattering glass and each shard scored her heart.

Daniel? It couldn't be. Not after all these years. Her heart beat too fast as she tried to see past the sea of heads. Her hands grew cold and clammy as she instinctively threaded her way through the people packed into the room. She needed to see. She needed to touch. She needed to know. An eerie, familiar melody buzzed inside her brain, simultaneously taking her back and begging her to go forward.

As if in answer to the echo of her past, the music started.

Unique.

Unmistakable.

Daniel.

Goose bumps skated up and down her arms. The room swirled in dizzying eddies of colors. Spirals of hope and despair had her struggling for breath. And like a dam overcome with melting snow, a flood of memories gushed, nearly taking her feet from under her.

Daniel.

Her hand sought support and found an arm. *"Mademoiselle?"*

Shaking her head, she snapped her hand away and gulped in air to stem the raging tide of panic surging through her. Slowly, the room stopped spinning, her breath returned to normal and her numbed brain started to function.

She parted the sea of adoring females that crowded around the piano, hanging on to every chord he cajoled from the instrument.

His hands came into view. Hands that had the long fingers of an artist. The well-toned muscles between the knuckles bore witness to the hours of practice. Her skin heated at their remembered touch. She readjusted her position. To get a better view. Nothing else.

When she caught sight of his profile, her stomach rebelled, washing waves of acid against its sides. Hand fisted against the pain, she fought to clear the flash from the past superimposing a younger man over this musician's features.

Her Daniel had been positively skinny, whereas this man had a supple leanness about him. Her Daniel had sported long, unkempt, sun-bleached hair, instead of this man's rich brown neatly cut style. Her Daniel's angular, intense face had pleased her. She searched the uncompromising lines of this man's face and found it hard to believe they were the same person.

There was no softness left in him. Instead, there was a primal quality about the way he played—as if he were darkness condensed and controlled, his emotions caged and doled out precisely for a choreographed response, his motions smooth and graceful, yet ordered and precise. There was no doubt he mastered the instrument.

She shivered.

Yet something was missing. Something that had once stirred her so deeply she'd broken all of her self-imposed rules.

Her Daniel had played with unbridled passion, the wildness a joy to watch. This Daniel played with soul, but without heart.

When he lifted his gaze, he found hers as if he'd known all along she would be there. She saw no apology in his eyes, no awkwardness, only clear, deep amber. For an instant the color smoldered intimately to intoxicating brandy, then it hardened, giving him an aloof expression that struck her as sadness disguised.

When the music stopped, people crowded around him like theater curtains, obscuring him from her view. She didn't fight the sweep. She let it separate her from him because she'd long ago put aside all her silly notions of a happy reunion. Instead, she'd spent her energy on forging a future for herself and her daughter. She was content with her choices. Daniel was her past.

It was time to leave. Time to get back to Rosane.

"CHRISTIANE!"

Fingers curled around her nearly bare shoulder,

stopping her. Daniel had a strong grasp that managed to be as gentle as a caress, yet left her no room to dismiss him. His touch shivered all the way up to her scalp, all the way down to her toes. No wonder he could play so well if a simple touch could shake her so.

"Daniel." Christi pasted a wide smile on her mouth as she turned to face him. Could a face crack from trying too hard to look relaxed? "How nice to see you again."

What did you say to an ex-lover after nine years? *Hi, and by the way, you left a little more of yourself than you thought when you took off. Yep, that's right, you're a daddy. I'd have told you much sooner, but you didn't leave a forwarding address.*

There was no good way to deliver this news. She toyed with the idea of keeping the secret to herself. Why should she upset three ordered lives?

Because she, of all people, understood he had the right to know. She would tell him. But not now, not tonight. Not with the shock of seeing him still ebbing from her body.

The quartet struck up again, playing a generic waltz that faded into the background along with the happy chatter and clink of glasses.

"Dance with me." There was a touch of vulnerability beneath the cutting steel of his voice, and she was tempted to let him lead her to the floor, to see if the electric passion that had burned them both still flickered. But that was a dangerous game, and she had Rosane to think of now.

"I was just leaving." Her gaze cut over his shoulder in search of Armand.

"So early? Dance with me, Christiane."

His voice was deeper, more resonant than she remembered, his presence more domineering, and his penetrating gaze caused bubbles of acid to pop in her stomach. "Another time, maybe. I have…obligations. I really have to go."

He grasped her elbow in one hand and turned her toward the cleared floor where a dozen couples waltzed. Talons would have been easier to dislodge.

"You don't want to cause a scene," he whispered in her ear. To anyone the gesture would have looked as if he were whispering sweet nothings.

His thumb caressed her elbow, gentling his insistence, short-circuiting the logical part of her brain. One dance, what could it hurt?

"Dance with me." His harsh gaze softened for an instant, and she saw the awkward boy once more— the one who'd stumbled over his words when he'd asked if he could walk her home after her shift at the ice-cream parlor.

She wasn't a teenager anymore; she could resist those eyes, that smile. Throat too dry to speak, she nodded and let him lead her onto the dance floor. One dance. She'd prove she was over him to them both.

The warmth of his hand on the small of her back penetrated the thin material of her dress and made her feel exposed. As he drew her closer, more potent heat radiated from him, making her trip over her own shadow. He'd once made a cold February night sizzle. As he steadied her, she closed her eyes, willing her body to forget the sensations her mind too easily remembered. Memories rippled up from their safe hiding place, and she braced against their assault.

"Relax," Daniel whispered. The ruffle of his

breath made her quiver. "I won't hurt you. I just want to talk to you."

"You played well tonight."

"Do you know my work?" Daniel skillfully skirted around another couple.

"No, other than Céline Dion, I don't know of any French Canadian stars who've made the news in Fort Worth." *I had no idea if you were dead or alive.* "I'm glad you realized your dream." God, she'd attended too many business affairs if she could talk to him that casually without falling apart.

"And you? Have your dreams come true?"

"Some." She shrugged, keeping her gaze averted from the liquid amber that had drawn too much out of her already. She didn't want to tell him about Rosane until she'd found firm footing again.

"Which ones?" His gaze measured her as they danced, making her wonder at the thoughts behind the rigid panes of his eyes.

To make matters worse, someone's stare pierced her spine. When she turned to look, it wasn't the envious ogling of another woman that caught her attention, but Armand's dark gaze. It lifted to meet Daniel's, then a satisfied smile curved his lips.

Daniel's arm tightened around her in a protective gesture. With an unexpected twirl, he guided her deeper into the fray of dancers.

"Do you know him?" she asked.

"Armand Langelier. I know him." His mouth thinned into a grimace as if the name tasted bitter.

"How do you know Armand?" Speaking with Daniel had always been an art, a matter of asking the questions, then reading the body as well as listening to the nuances between the words. Discussing his emotions had appeared an impossible task. This trait hadn't improved with age.

Without warning, Daniel stood still though the music hadn't stopped. Dancing couples brushed against them. An unfathomable darkness crossed his face. His jaw tightened. He stared at Armand through the crowd. For an instant his expression was filled with a mixture of regret and pain so deep it weighed on her heart.

"He used to be a well-respected lawyer. It's said he helped form many happy families." Bitterness underlined his words. Abruptly, Daniel's arms fell away from her body and his hand gripped hers. "Come, let me take you home."

With long-legged strides, he started for the door. Her hand firmly trapped in his, she had no choice but to follow. What was Daniel's connection to Armand? A total stranger didn't warrant such a strong reaction.

"Slow down." Christi tried to slip her hand from his. "I came with someone else."

"We have to talk."

"You had your chance while we were dancing."

"It wasn't a suggestion, Christiane. Your life is at stake."

"My life?" She scoffed at his exaggeration. "Aren't you being overdramatic?"

"We need to talk."

She skidded to a halt, forcing Daniel to do the same. Her free hand tightened into a fist, her stomach clenched into a squirming knot and the rising heat of anger had sweat breaking out along her hairline. A glass from a passing waiter's tray swayed, then fell, taking its neighbors with it like bowling pins. Champagne splashed down the side of her dress.

She stood tree still, staring first at the broken pieces of glass at her feet, then at the dark stain running down the side of her dress. As a glimmer of something forgotten sparked, then faded, the blood drained from her limbs, leaving her skin ice-cold and prickling.

With effluent apologies, the waiter dabbed at her dress with a linen napkin, picked up the broken pieces scattered around her satin pumps and retreated.

Christi looked at Daniel and surprised herself with her calmness. "I can't leave without telling my escort and thanking our hostess."

"I'll get our coats while you make our goodbyes."

"You're the guest of honor. You have to stay."

A sardonic twist crooked his smile. "Musicians are eccentric, don't you know? Madame Bernier is a good friend. She'll understand. I will thank her profusely tomorrow."

His eyes held a warning, one that spoke of danger in refusal, surging question after question, the chief one being—what was going on?

Chapter Two

"Marry you?"

The hard drum of Christi's heart slapped against her ears, making her wonder for a moment if she'd hallucinated the words she'd heard. An hour ago she hadn't known Daniel was alive, and now, here in her mother's childhood home, he was asking her to spend the rest of her life with him? "Just like that?"

Only the fluorescent fixture over the sink lit the room. Its stark light stretched the shadows of the pine table and chairs to horror film proportions. The black window skewed its reflection of the kitchen out of shape. Only hours ago, she'd found comfort here, and Daniel was taking it all away.

He slung his midnight-colored coat, tuxedo jacket and bow tie onto the back of the nearest kitchen chair. "Yes. Just like that."

Feeling every one of Quebec City's twenty degrees below zero as if the room had no insulation, no walls, Christi buried her hands deep into her coat pockets to keep them warm.

Part of her had waited so long to hear those words. Yet a sense of disappointment, of confusion, rather than joy filled her. She'd wanted to hear the words, but not in this dispassionate way. That wasn't the Daniel she knew and loved.

Had loved. She swallowed hard. Still loved. The truth hit hard. Her fist automatically sought the hard lump in her stomach, trying to soothe it with massaging pressure. As much as she'd like to hate him, as much as she'd like to pretend the love had melted along with the anger, she couldn't. In spite of all that had happened, in spite of the fact they were hardly more than strangers, she still cared for him in a way that defied all logic.

"Would you like some tea or coffee?" Daniel asked with the ease of someone who was at home. Ease he shouldn't have felt in the house that belonged to her mother's cousin.

"No." She breathed the word out on a long exhale and took her time to fill her lungs once more. "I don't want tea. I don't want coffee. What I do want is answers."

"Some things are better left unsaid."

"Like goodbye?"

A muscle flinched in his jaw, but otherwise, he gave no indication her deliberate barb had found its mark.

He opened a set of cupboard doors and rummaged through the contents on the shelves. "And if you don't like the answers, Christiane, what will you do?"

"I'll survive. I've done it often enough." Raised as an air force brat, she'd left enough friends behind to learn how to cope with constant changes.

He banged the cupboard doors closed and moved to the next set. "The answer is that you've walked into a long-standing battle between me and Armand. If you stay here, you'll only get hurt."

"I've already been hurt." And the way he'd left cut the deepest wound. If she'd survived that, she could survive anything.

Holding on to the glass handles, Daniel pressed his forehead against the crack between the crisp white cupboard doors. The signs were all there. She recognized the thin edge of control he held on his temper, the explosive emotions caged somewhere beneath the surface, and imagined the jumble of words hurtling chaotically in his head never to be spoken.

"If you hate Armand so much, how come you have a key to his house?"

"My father was his business partner. He was once a friend of the family. He was my godfather."

She nodded once, sensing the ties made the battle between them that much more potent, but not quite understanding them, or why she was caught in the middle.

"Why?" She was aware of him on a physical level. Aware of the space he occupied, of the tension in his shoulders, of the uncomprehending way she wanted to go to him and hold him. She tried to look past all the layers of armor he'd suited himself with, reaching out for the missing something behind the words. The past and present mingled until she wasn't quite sure where she was. So she focused on the curiously vulnerable bend of his neck. "Why do you want to marry me?"

Slowly, he turned to face her. He leaned the heels of his hands on the gray-flecked counter. His gaze met hers with control ruling. "Since you refuse to leave, it's the only way I can think to protect you."

"I don't need protection." *I need* you.

"I can give you now what I couldn't offer you then."

"That's it?" She shook her head. A cold sadness squeezed her heart. She'd wanted something from him, but not that.

"What more do you want?" Without waiting for an answer, he turned back to the cupboard, and with quick movements, returned to his hunt.

"What about love?" Her voice sounded thin and stretched with desperation. As if her index finger belonged to someone else, she watched it trace a smooth knot on the table's pine board.

"What of it?"

"You're offering marriage." She twitched her finger off the table when she realized the knot on the pine board was shaped like a lopsided heart. "Does it include love?"

"Love is a useless emotion." He found a jar of instant coffee and banged it on the counter. He whisked a mug from a display shelf on the side of the sink window and set it beside the coffee jar with a thump. "We're adults now, not children. We're old enough to know that feelings have no place in this world."

"What's the point of marriage, then?"

"You said you wanted roots."

Her heart hitched inside her chest. He'd remembered that from their six-month courtship? Her gaze sought him and she willed him to turn around.

He twisted the sink's spigot too harshly and water splashed onto his white tuxedo shirt. Without acknowledging the wetness, he stuffed the kettle under the water's stream and filled it. "I can protect you. I can give you security. I can give you the world."

"But not your love." She no longer seemed to feel anything—not the room's cold air, not the fire in her stomach, not the feelings that should be ripping through her like a tornado.

"There are more solid things between a man and a woman than useless feelings."

"Like what?" Could he have forgotten the passion they'd once shared?

He jammed the kettle onto a burner and wrenched the knob. The *click-click-click* of spark kindling gas sounded like cockroaches scurrying for cover. "Like the things you say you want, Christiane. Family, roots, security."

Her voice could not climb up her throat. A tiny sound echoed inside her like a wounded cry. She checked her cheeks with a quick flick of her hand to make sure no moisture stained them, betraying the ease with which he could tear open old wounds.

"Trust me." He said the words so softly, she had to strain to catch them. Their gazes met and held. His weighty sadness mixed with hers and wove a bond of regret for all that might have been, all that could never be.

"The last time I trusted you," she blurted out, "I ended up alone and pregnant."

She hadn't meant to tell him. Not now. Not like this. As she waited for his reaction, no air could crawl through the constricted passages of her lungs. Her fingers dug into the soft flesh of her stomach, trying to stem the flickers of fire burning through her gut. Nothing moved across his face. No shadow, no emotion, no surprise. He was taking the news of his fatherhood as if she'd casually mentioned the weather—calmly, much too calmly. Could he really feel so little?

"Then think of our child." If he'd said anything else. If he hadn't said the words so blankly. If he hadn't looked at her with such remote coldness, she could have kept her cool. But his utter lack of emotion detonated a small explosion deep inside her, one that concentrated all he should have felt with all she couldn't contain and spewed it out in a high, thin voice. "Our child? *Our* child!" She thumped her fist against her chest. "My child, Daniel. *My* daughter."

"Mine also. An obligation it's past time I take on."

Anger snaked into rampant fear as his unspoken threat unleashed a forewarning so terrifying she was at a loss for words.

"It's my right to know my daughter." He snagged a spoon from a jelly jar on the table, catching the lip of the glass.

Her hands gnarled into fists. Her muscles shook with such intensity she had to clamp her arms at her sides to keep herself from leaping out of her chair. She barely registered when the spoon jar rattled against the table, when it toppled over, scattering spoons onto the tabletop, spilling them onto the floor, when the falling spoons clacked like skeleton teeth against the linoleum tiles. "You. Can't. Have. Her." *She's all I have.*

Carefully, he dropped a heaping spoonful of instant coffee into a mug and laid the spoon on the counter. Precisely, he screwed the plastic cap back onto the glass jar. Rigidly, he replaced the jar into the cupboard, giving a half twist so the red and gold label would face out like the rest of the bottles and jars on the shelf. "If you want to stay here, you'll have to do it on my terms."

"You have no hold on me." Barely aware she was moving, she rose. "I won't let you play with me, hurt me again." With slow, purposeful steps, she moved toward him. "I won't let you use my daughter to control me."

He started forward with cool, measured strides, meeting her halfway. They stood facing each other squarely, a foot of space between them—two hungry dogs, one precious bone. "You're not giving me any choice. I need—"

"You need what, Daniel? *Tell me.*"

He crowded in on her, invading her personal space with the intensity of his will, his heat, his body. She backed away reflexively. Playing with fire was dangerous. He followed, matching her step for step. She was going to get burned. He backed her against the solid surface of the refrigerator. And there was no way out.

"There's too much between us." His voice, low and husky, rumbled through her. "Bonds. Obligations. History." He planted the back of one hand next to her head on the refrigerator's enamel and fanned the tips of his fingers through the ends of her hair. "By insisting on staying, you're bringing the past into the present. You're asking for loose ends to be tied."

Loose ends. The edge of madness dissipated. Loose ends. She hadn't thought of it that way, but it was. Her history was a loose end. Daniel was a loose end. She herself was a loose end. And he was right. Loose ends needed trimming.

He reached for her then, his free hand molding to the back of her neck, fingertips burrowing between

strands of her hair to cradle the sensitive scalp beneath. She trembled at his touch, felt the echo of it
shimmer through him. He pressed his lips against
hers, savoring, caressing, demanding a response. He
tasted hot and exciting, and she couldn't help the
throaty sound of desire as she opened up to him. His
hand skimmed her shoulder, followed the curve of her
back to her waist and pressed her closer to him, letting
her feel him come alive against her. Her skin warmed.
Her blood heated. Her pulse flared. Against her will,
she softened against him, melting with a sigh into his
embrace, responding to his unexpected male hunger
with a feminine fierceness that surprised her.

He knew her. Knew how to play her with even
more ease than his keyboard. Knew she could not
resist him anymore than she could resist his music.
And he would take away the only point of stability
in her life. All to get what he wanted.

"Please...stop." Struggling, she pushed away from
the blaze of his kiss with a trembling hand.

He allowed her a small retreat, but held her hips
prisoner in his palms. "You wanted me then. You
want me still. It's a solid enough base for a marriage."

"I let you into my bed because I loved you, not to
satisfy hormones. Sex isn't solid. It's a moment."

"A moment you've lived with for nine years." His
thumb glided gently over her still-moist bottom lip.
Her skin pulsated in the trail of his touch. The shadow
of memories played on his face, softening the harsh
lines around his mouth, deepening the amber of his
eyes to that mellow brandy that made her forget logic.
"Can you honestly say that you don't want me?"

Still and always. "You hurt me once. I won't let you hurt me again."

But physical love wasn't enough. She wanted more—she wanted permanence. She needed an emotional connection, too—soil that would allow roots to grow deep and strong. And he wasn't prepared to give her that. She needed to release the lingering something between them. Only then would she be free to go on with the rest of her life without the tug of nostalgia.

The kettle's water, spilling over the red-hot burner, hissed, diverting his attention. As he released her, a mixture of regret and relief scrambled through her, drawing a long exhale of breath. No other man could run up her temperature so high and so fast. He'd once made her feel safe and loved. He'd once made her believe in forever. And it had all turned out to be illusion. Hands pressed against the refrigerator's humming surface, she became aware of the returning acid storm in her stomach.

Daniel made a near ritual of filling his mug with water and stirring his coffee more vigorously than necessary before he turned to face her. "There's something between us that even nine years hasn't erased. Armand's counting on that. He'll use it, Christiane, and destroy us both."

"I don't understand." She rubbed at the chill permeating the thick layer of her coat.

"And I don't know how to explain it."

She leaned forward, drawing her arms tight under her chest, pleading. *Talk to me.* "Try."

"Armand wants something from you."

"What? What could an old man possibly want from me?"

Daniel took a hasty sip from his mug, then grimaced as the hot liquid burned his tongue. "I'm not sure." He slammed the mug down. Coffee spilled over the side, steamed in a ghostlike breath, then pooled on the counter. "But by sticking together we have a better chance of defeating him than by standing alone being played one against the other. Whatever else you do, you have to trust me. I won't let anyone hurt you."

Except you. You'll hurt me, Daniel.

A piece in a game. That's what he'd called her earlier. The stakes for her—her identity, her heart, her daughter. Whether she stayed or left, she risked everything. For him? A question mark, and no enlightenment on the horizon.

Would he really use Rosane against her? Was it fair to keep Rosane away from her father and keep her from knowing her roots? It was, after all, what Christi sought for herself. Maybe if she allowed Daniel to see Rosane, he would understand it was better if he didn't upset their ordered lives.

She huffed a ragged sigh. A headache echoed the pain searing her stomach. "You've the right to know your daughter, and she, you. But promise me something, Daniel—"

"Anything."

"Promise you won't try to take her away from me under any circumstance."

"I'll do anything to keep you both safe."

"Promise me," she insisted. "I need to hear the words."

From across the kitchen, the harsh light above the sink cut his face with grim shadows and rigid lines.

But the amber of his eyes was clear and vibrant. ''I promise.''

The solid timbre of his voice, the unbending look in his eyes, the shred of soul reaching out to her told her he would do everything he could to keep his word. Part of the storm inside her ebbed. ''Thank you.''

She pushed herself off the refrigerator's surface and stuffed her hands deep into her coat pockets. ''I need time…to tell Rosane about you.'' Christi lifted her shoulders and shook her head.

His cup halted midway to his mouth. ''What's wrong?''

''Nothing's wrong.'' Christi lowered her gaze to the black and white checkerboard of tiles on the floor, then raised it again. ''She thinks her father's dead.'' An almost imperceptible flinch flashed through his eyes. ''I'm sorry. But in a way, you were dead to both of us. Please. Give me time to prepare her.''

He nodded curtly. ''I'll give you a week.''

''It may not be enough.''

''One week, Christiane.'' He stamped his cup against the counter with impatience. ''Then you'll have to marry me and let me take my rightful place in her life. Or you'll have to leave.''

Leaving would be easier. A short-term remedy for a long-time ill. But marrying him wasn't a decision she was ready to make in such a short time. And with her parents recently dead, she'd lost too much to turn back with no answers. If a friend had come to her with this dilemma, she'd have counseled her to stay, to see things through. She had a week—a lot could happen in a week. ''I'll tell Rosane about you. But I can't marry you. Not when you refuse to tell me what's going on between you and Armand and why you think my life is in danger.''

Daniel grabbed a rag from a hook inside the cupboard door beneath the sink, then wiped the coffee spill. He plopped the wet rag into the sink. ''If Armand invited you here, he has a reason. And it's not your well-being.''

''What other reason could there be?''

Taking a sip from his mug, he leaned against the counter and crossed his ankles. ''Did you know I was the guest of honor at the gala tonight?''

''No, I—''

''Armand conveniently forgot to mention the fact because it suited him to make a point.''

''But—''

''There's no *but,* Christiane. Armand is the devil himself. He invited you here to continue what he started nine years ago.'' He held up a hand to halt the question about to spill out of her mouth. ''He found you nine years ago through me. He wanted something then. I don't know what, only that it scared your mother and made me abandon my music scholarship. I wanted to protect you then, Christiane, and I want to protect you now. He invited me here to let me know I had no control over the outcome. I won't let him win.'' Frustration strained his face. ''Do you understand?''

''No, I don't.'' Points to be made? Devils in disguise? Covert plans and schemes? Daniel was wrong. Armand had nothing to gain from her. Daniel was turning this once warm kitchen into a deep freeze of suspicion where half truths fogged the air. ''What has Armand done to you to make you hate him so?''

"He treated me like a son. Then he betrayed my—me."

"How? What happened?"

For a long time, Daniel simply stared at her. She wanted to go to him, shake him, punch him, do something, anything to let the words locked in his skull spill out. But she did nothing, except stare back, and wait for the words she knew wouldn't come.

"What's important now is keeping you safe," he said.

Enough was enough. He wanted to play with smoke and mirrors, and she wanted straight answers. They weren't going to get anywhere at this rate. If he couldn't explain, then she couldn't accept the notion of Armand as a threat. She wasn't going to let Daniel put down the only solace she'd felt in a long time.

"Armand and Marguerite have been nothing but kind and generous. They've given me something I've been looking for since I was a little girl. A sense of where I come from, where I belong."

Even on the other side of the room, Daniel crowded her. "You belong with me."

She placed both her hands on the table separating them and challenged him. "Then why did you leave?"

"I told you. To keep you safe. I had no choice."

As she straightened her stance, she let out a short, sharp laugh. "No choice, no heart, no love. Where does that leave me, Daniel? I'll tell you where. It leaves me hanging and I don't like that. I've had too much of that in my life. It has to end."

The turbulent mix of emotions churning through her was too much. She needed time to think, time to sort through all the questions, time to let her rioting feelings settle. "Well, it's been an interesting evening, but I'm tired." She ran a hand through her hair. "If you'll excuse me, I'm going to check on my daughter and go to bed." She walked stiffly to the kitchen door and turned. She gripped the door frame with a force that sapped the blood from her fingertips, leaving them white. "I trust you can see yourself out."

"It's not going to end this simply."

"It can."

"Armand's already played his next move." Daniel swallowed another sip of coffee. "I've been invited."

"Invited?"

"Here. As a guest."

"Then bid your fond regrets. If he's playing a game, who says you have to follow his rules?"

"There's too much at stake. I need to keep you safe. We have a daughter. Obligations."

With one hand she grandly made the sign of the cross. "I absolve you from them all."

"Not this time." Both his hands tightened around the mug. "Marry me, Christiane." His voice bore a strangely insistent urgency.

Her smile was forced. She was a fool. He would never love her. And she couldn't help loving the boy who'd painted her dull world with rich music and vibrant passion, the boy who'd made her believe she could belong. Expectations would only lead to heartache. But to sever the ties, she had to find out how deeply they ran. In her. In him. So she reached out.

"Do you remember when I told you about the moon?" She'd let herself become vulnerable. She'd told him about her anchor in an ever-changing world. And he'd told her she didn't have to look that far. In his eyes, in his kiss, in his lovemaking, she'd heard his unspoken promise. He'd become her anchor, her moon.

"Yes."

"Make me believe, Daniel. Make me believe."

AFTER CHRISTIANE left the room, Daniel dumped the bitter coffee down the sink. He hated instant. He hated having to push Christiane. But mostly, he hated how hard he'd become. He looked down at the black star sapphire ring he wore on his right hand. Just like his father.

Though the ring was a reminder his soul was tainted, he had a measure of hope for Christiane. As he'd kissed her, he'd sensed the remnants of a bond forged long ago between them, sensed it reignite. If he could fan it into life, strengthen it, then maybe he could save her from whatever twisted scheme poisoned Armand's mind. He'd done it once when he'd given up his scholarship to buy her freedom; he could do it again.

Distractedly, he rinsed the cup and placed it in the sink. He'd spent the past nine years trying to make amends for his choices. Everyone he'd tried to protect had ended up hurt anyway—Christiane, his mother, his sister…his daughter.

With a careless swoop, he grabbed his coat, jacket and tie from the back of the chair. Five years ago his music had finally paid off and allowed him to buy his mother the art gallery she'd always wanted and help his sister set up her family practice. Which left the debt he owed Christiane and their child.

Turning off the kitchen light, he stepped into the darkened hall. The memories of his feelings for Christiane had tortured him for years. He had no desire to reexperience that agony. Not when he'd finally come to terms with his life.

He would make a good husband, take care of Christiane and their daughter, provide a safe home for them. She'd have her roots. He'd have his career. They'd both have their daughter. They could carry off this marriage with polite civility. The physical bond was enough. He'd see to that. Why complicate the whole thing with useless feelings that only got in the way?

Look what had happened the last time he'd let anything touch his heart. He'd lost everything he'd cared for. He'd found out Armand had used him to get to Christiane, that Armand had tried to kill Christiane's mother years earlier and caused her to flee in fear, that the only way to protect Christiane from suffering her mother's fate was to leave her behind and give up his coveted Van Cliburn scholarship.

Except that it was too easy to let down his guard around Christiane, to let her passion fuel his, to forget he'd made a bargain with the devil and that the prize was her life.

As he wound his way through the familiar corridors, he shook off the sense of dread creeping into his bones. The last time he'd walked through this house, he'd sentenced himself to hell. What would his presence here cost him this time?

At the foot of the stairs, he heard the whisper of Christiane's voice wishing their daughter sweet dreams, the smack of lips against fingers as she blew her a kiss. With an unexpected fierceness, the memory of Christiane's kiss ratcheted through him. One kiss had cartwheeled him back to sharing sundaes, moonlit car rides and a pile of blankets under a star-studded sky. One kiss had him wishing for a house in the woods filled with music and laughter and family.

He snapped on the light just inside the sitting room's French door and pushed the door with enough force to close it just shy of a slam. He'd had no more time to prepare this time than the last. But now, his power and influence were equal to Armand's. He would not cave.

He dropped his coat, jacket and tie onto the plum-upholstered, spindly-legged chair by the door. Having Christiane here was more complicated than he'd expected. He could have dealt with hate. Indifference— even better.

But she'd asked him for the moon.

He choked out a rough bark. The one thing she wanted from him was the only thing he couldn't give her. For both their sakes. His control over the darkness was precarious at best. If he let her into his heart, they were both doomed.

He poured himself generous fingers of scotch from Armand's finest stock, then slumped into the chair next to the gaping maw of the hearth. Leaning his head back, he propped his feet on the kidney-shaped coffee table.

"To you, old man." He raised his glass to the glacial chill of the empty room. "And to your defeat."

But there was no satisfaction in the promise, only the sure knowledge of inevitable death. The liquor he swallowed didn't warm him. Nothing would. Not until he discovered Armand's plans and knew how to keep Christiane safe.

An insistent cacophony jangled in the back of his mind, proving that chaos was only a step away. He closed his eyes and let the notes flow through his brain. They arranged and rearranged themselves into a familiar pattern. He sighed as he recognized the melody. Music had dragged him from the black edge of hell twice. Could it manage the feat a third time?

Unable to resist, he went to the piano and let his fingers dance over the keys.

"Maybe tonight…"

For years the melancholic notes had tormented him. Taunting him when he was tired and his defenses were down. Letting the piece run its course was the only way to get rid of it. Tonight he added a few notes, but still the end wouldn't come.

Like this melody that wouldn't finish itself, Christiane was unfinished business.

He'd tried letting her go. Now he would try hanging on to her.

Tumbling the piano bench backwards, he stood. With a stiff motion, he reached for his glass and drained the rest of the scotch, taking pleasure in the liquor's caustic burn down his throat. Again he raised this glass to the cold room. "One more time—without feeling."

Chapter Three

Christi needed a few moments to orient herself when she woke up the next morning. As the room focused around her, she remembered where she was and sighed. Daniel's apparition last night had ruined her joy at finding her mother's family.

Strong light filtered through the open moiré draperies, but the house was deathly silent and a slow dread snaked its way from her stomach to her throat. The last thing she wanted to do today was face Daniel again or confess a truth she'd hidden for much too long to her daughter. Both would cost her what little balance she had left in her life.

She reached for her watch on the night table. "Eight-fifteen! Ugh."

She let herself flop back onto the bed. After last night, she could use a couple more hours of sleep. Given her scrambled state of mind, she was surprised she'd slept at all.

Her gaze wandered over the room. But it wasn't the carved walnut furniture, the Aubusson rug or the cream lace coverlet that caught her eye. It was her grandmother's portrait near the rocking chair in the corner. Catherine Langelier. Armand had told Christi that the silver brush set on the dresser was Catherine's. And if she closed her eyes, Christi swore she could smell the trace of her grandmother's rose-scented perfume lingering on the lace runner on the vanity.

She let her imagination roam until a weathered woman formed out of the mists of her musings. She sat at the vanity, wearing an old-fashioned white satin robe that was rich, yet demure. A delicate gold chain draped the creases of her neck, the pendant hidden beneath the neckline of her gown. A blue jar of cold cream stood next to a gold-cased lipstick and a fancy bottle of perfume. Light refracted into a rainbow as it passed through the bottle's long, prism-shaped top. The woman sat stroking her long white hair with the silver brush. And in a trick of reverie, it seemed to Christi as if the woman looked straight at her through the mirror and smiled.

Christi shook her head. The image faded away. "I must be more tired than I thought. Damn you Daniel for showing up at the wrong place at the wrong time and screwing up my life again." But the last part wasn't fair. If she didn't have feelings for him, she could have gone on as if nothing had happened between them.

Masks. She'd kept too many of them in her makeup bag over the years. It was time to strip them off and find out who she really was and what she was really made of. That would mean taking risks. Would Rosane hate her when she found out the truth about her father? Was there any chance they could all breach those nine years and become a real family? Was marriage to Daniel, even on his terms, such a bad thing?

Her job as the public relations manager of a small

cable television station in Fort Worth had trained her
to make decisions on the spot and stick by them. But
there she wore her public mask; she could keep an
objective distance. Now her decision would alter her
life permanently. And the last thing she wanted was
to lose more than she already had.

As soon as Christi flipped back the blankets, the
room's frigid air assaulted her. She'd seen signs of
central heat, but for some reason, the warm air didn't
seem to reach this part of the stone house. She rubbed
her arms and reached into the suitcase on the bench
at the foot of the bed for a sweater.

Rosane should be up by now.

Christi peeked through the door across the hall.

"Rosie?"

There was no answer. The bed was neatly made.
There were no signs of her daughter anywhere.

"No!" The "what ifs" galloped through her mind
like a car without brakes. What if Daniel was still
here? What if he'd taken Rosane? What if he'd told
her who he was before Christi had a chance to prepare
her?

"Calm down. She's perfectly all right. Daniel
promised you a week." But the image of Daniel's
determined face came flashing back into her mind.
His demand wasn't a whim, but a wish he fully in-
tended to fulfill.

Feet bare and with only her blue flannel nightgown
and red sweater on, she rushed down the stairs. "Rosane! Rosie, where are you?"

Christi jerked to a halt at the bottom of the stairs.
A childish giggle warbled from the kitchen. Like a
hound on a scent, she followed the sound. And when

she reached the kitchen, she didn't know what to make of what she saw.

Rosane, already dressed in a purple sweatshirt and jeans, heaped spoonfuls of Cap'n Crunch into her mouth and giggled. Her daughter who rarely smiled was giggling with glee. One of Christi's hands instinctively reached for her stomach; the other covered her mouth.

The gray eyes behind those long lashes were like her own. The rich golden brown hair spilling over her shoulders was like her mother's. The long artistic fingers curled around the spoon were Daniel's legacy. Christi saw the past in her daughter. A past that wound down for generations. Generations she knew nothing about. Daniel was wrong, staying here was right.

Armand entertained Rosane by making a dollar coin appear and disappear from midair. Marguerite, roly-poly like the plastic people Rosane used to play with as a toddler, puttered at the counter. From all indications, the woman seemed to live in the kitchen. Christi hadn't seen her anywhere else. Daniel, she noted with relief, was nowhere in sight.

The kitchen's warmth contrasted keenly with the coldness of the rest of the house. The table of whitewashed pine and the six matching chairs with their red gingham cushions provided a homey atmosphere out of character with the stiff, formal furnishings in the rest of the house. In daylight, she could almost convince herself her conversation with Daniel was just a bad dream.

Rosane tucked a lock of hair behind her ear and squinted at Armand. "Hey! How come you're squeaking?"

Armand lifted his arms and opened his eyes wide in innocence. The spreading warmth of his smile softened the harsh angles of his thin face. The pleasure, when Rosane squealed with delight as he pulled a kitten from his jacket, was genuine. Daniel was wrong. Armand had no evil motives. Rosane forgot about the forbidden sugared cereal and lavished love on the squirming gray kitten.

"Is it a boy or a girl?" Rosane asked, leaning back from a cheek cleaning by the kitten's sandpaper tongue.

Armand lifted the kitten's tail. "I believe it is a girl."

"Can I keep her?"

"She is especially for you."

Rosane let out a jubilant shriek and hugged the kitten to her chest.

"What are you going to name her?" Armand lifted his coffee cup and his sister filled it for him.

Rosane's face scrunched in concentration. "Something French. How do you say smoke?"

"Fumée."

"Few-may." As the kitten's rough tongue scraped her nose, Rosane giggled again. "It's a good name. She looks like a puff of smoke, don't you think? Fumée. I like that."

A pang of envy knocked around Christi's chest at the ease with which Armand had made Rosane feel at home and at his ability to wrest smiles out of her. Not the devil, she thought, a magician.

"Armand, *pas à la table*," Marguerite chided. Her round glasses magnified her black eyes, making them the most prominent feature on her moon face. "The child has to eat."

"Let her have some fun."

"She is not yours to spoil," she said in French.

"It is no worse than all the junk you are stuffing her with."

Marguerite waved his retort away with a dimpled hand. "*Non,* it's not the same."

Armand leaned back in his chair and gazed at Rosane with adoration. "She's perfect, *n'est ce pas?*"

"*Diable,* Armand! She is just a child," Marguerite insisted, jamming a strand of gray hair back into its tight bun.

"She looks like Caro, don't you think? Only she is much stronger. You can tell by the way she carries herself and the depth in those eyes."

Marguerite harrumphed and slammed shut the refrigerator door. She filled a saucer with milk and set it next to Rosane's cereal bowl. She wiped her hands on the pristine white apron cinched over her plain, out-of-date black dress. In broken English, she said, "Maybe Fumée have hunger."

Rosane set the kitten down. It lapped contentedly at the milk. "She does. Look at her go!"

"Do you like the flavor of maple?" A conspiratorial smile animated Marguerite's starched face.

It was as if they were trying to outdo each other to gain Rosane's affection. A smile sneaked up on Christi. Family wanting to fit together, wanting to be liked. There's no evil in that.

"I love it!" Rosane stroked the kitten as if it were made of glass. "Mom always buys the real thing even though it's more expensive. It's much better than that fake syrup stuff."

"Try this." Marguerite placed two pieces of toast before Rosane. They oozed with a spread the pale sand of maple sugar. "I think you not have Map-O-Spread at Texas."

Rosane took a healthy bite and nodded her approval. "This is good. Mom never lets me have sugar stuff for breakfast. Except for pancakes on Sunday sometimes."

Christi pressed her fingers tighter against her lip to silence her laughter. She'd gone from junk food queen to Mother Earth while she carried Rosane. The transformation had done wonders for her until her parents' death. Then all the old feelings of rootlessness returned with a punch, and with them, her stomach troubles. Had Rosane felt deprived? Guilt spiked an unwelcome wave of acid in her gut. Sometimes the creature she'd borne seemed so foreign to her.

Christi shook her head, pasted on her famous all's-right smile and marched into the kitchen.

"Well, you're cheerful this morning." Christi kissed the top of Rosane's head and ran her fingers through the soft strands of her daughter's hair.

"Look, Mom! Look what Armand gave me!" Rosane lifted the kitten up for inspection. "Can I keep her? Can I?"

How could she refuse Rosane anything when she looked so happy? "She can be yours while we're here."

"Oh, goodie!" Rosane rubbed her nose against the kitten's. "Did you hear that, Fumée? I get to keep you." She squeezed the kitten to her chest before turning the creature over on her lap to scratch the soft belly. The kitten nipped at the wiggly fingers, and Rosane giggled at their game.

Christi glanced at Marguerite, then at Armand. The kitchen's temperature seemed to drop a few degrees.

Was it her imagination or had the starched lines and stony expression reappeared on Marguerite's face?

"You slept well last night?" Smiling at her, Armand pushed away his cup of coffee. His slow gracious charm put her at ease as it had since she'd arrived two days ago.

"Yes, thank you."

"What can I make you for breakfast?" Marguerite asked in her halting English. Her gaze inspected Christi's attire and her frown disapproved.

"That's all right, you don't have to serve me. I'll help myself."

"I do not permit anyone to disturb my kitchen."

Then the coffee mess Daniel left last night must have tickled her pink this morning. "In that case, I'll have some tea." The odor of fresh-brewed coffee permeated the kitchen. Christi longed for a cup, but didn't think her stomach could handle it this morning.

"Orange Pekoe or *menthe?*"

"Mint is fine."

After she put the kettle on, Marguerite turned back to Christi. "What you like to eat?"

"Just toast, please." Christi didn't think she could manage anything else and the answer of "nothing" seemed unacceptable, judging from the disapproving scowl Marguerite leveled at her.

"That is all?"

Christi nodded. Acid lapped in her stomach. With a hand, she massaged her stormy stomach. "I must have eaten something that didn't agree with me at the party last night." She attempted a smile. "Thank you for keeping an eye on Rosane. I appreciate your kindness."

Marguerite harrumphed and returned to the stove.

Rosane slunk out of her chair to play on the floor with the kitten. She teased Fumée with a lock of her hair and the kitten batted at it with its paws.

Armand pulled a cigarette from his jacket pocket, lit it with a monogrammed gold lighter and puffed deeply. A moment later, a rheumy cough rattled in his chest. The stink of the smoke did nothing to improve Christi's appetite.

"I have a present for you, too."

"Oh, that's really not necessary—"

Armand reached behind him to the sideboard and picked up a thick album sheathed in burgundy leather. "I have found the photo album I told you about yesterday."

"You did!" Christi had never seen a picture of her mother as a child. And her mother had categorically refused to speak of her past. All of Christi's questions had remained unanswered, brushed aside like pesky fruit flies. As she scooted her chair closer to the table, anticipation warmed her.

A gold *L* was embossed on the cover. As he turned to the first page, the leather creaked. She wrinkled her nose at the scent of dust and history that rose into the air like fairy powder. He glided the album across the table until it rested between them. She wrapped her feet around the chair's legs and leaned in for a closer look.

"This is your grandmother, Catherine, and her husband, Henri." Armand seemed as eager to share the album's contents as she was to view them. "Henri died young—only a few years after your mother was born. Marguerite and I came to live with Catherine and Caroline soon after when our own parents were killed in a train accident."

"How awful!"

Although she could not mistake Catherine for Caroline, Christi noticed the strong resemblance between her grandmother and her mother, between her mother and herself. A quick glance at Rosane showed her the resemblance was passed on. Alike, yet so different.

Even the flicker of the imagined woman sitting at the vanity bore a certain likeness to the women in the album's pages. Had her tired mind invented a distant relative? With a shake of her head, Christi scattered the question and concentrated on Armand's stories.

"This one," he said, laughing easily as he pointed to a picture of her mother in a gauzy summer dress and a floppy hat, both soaked and dripping, "was taken after Caro insisted she could row the boat all by herself. She was very bossy even as a ten-year-old. The canoe tipped over as she got in and she fell into the lake."

Some things didn't change. Her mother had disguised an iron will with a soft voice. "And you were waiting with a camera?"

"Of course. I showed this photo to all her potential boyfriends. Until she took one of me in a rather ungraceful position after I had fallen while sledding."

As Armand told her stories of his youth, Marguerite placed a plate of scrambled eggs and ham next to her brother. He ignored it.

A vignette fell before Christi of places and people that were part of her, yet alien—a picnic with Catherine holding a young Caroline on her lap, Armand and Marguerite stood behind them, hamming it up for the camera. Birthday parties. Graduations. Vacations. Family together, sharing, feasting, laughing.

She drank in every detail. Each new glimpse into

her mother's world clicked a missing piece in the puzzle of her past into place. And with each space filled came a growing sense of a form wanting to finish itself.

Daniel was wrong. Armand didn't want to take anything from her. He wanted to give her what should have been hers all along.

Rosane climbed on Christi's knee for a while, commenting on the funny outfits in the pictures, but soon returned to the floor with her kitten.

As Armand closed the cover of the album, Christi sighed and sank contentedly against the back of her chair. "Thank you."

"It was my pleasure."

Leaving the album before her, he shook out a newspaper and puffed on a fresh cigarette. A moment later, the newspaper convulsed in time to a coughing fit.

Christi fingered the album's leather, loathe to sever her connection with her missing past.

Armand crumpled the newspaper beside his ignored plate of food. "Has your mother ever told you of the legend of Rose Latulippe?"

"No, she believed fairy tales were too violent for children."

"Pity." Armand took out a handkerchief and coughed into it. "It is such an interesting story about a young girl who danced with the devil on Mardi Gras." He returned the handkerchief to his pocket. "Did you know that legends have a basis in fact?"

"I've heard that." With slow movements of her index finger, Christi traced the gold *L* on the cover.

"One of your names is Rose, is it not?"

"Y-yes." Her finger hesitated on the downward curve of the *L.*

Armand's gaze drifted to Rosane who tested the kitten's pouncing skills with a piece of string. "Did you have a strong impulse to name her Rose?"

How could he know such a thing?

"And her father, was he not a handsome stranger?"

She gasped, snapping her finger from the album. "No, of course not." The quick denial was for Rosane's benefit.

Christi had woven her memories of Daniel into a mantle of fantasy for her daughter. She'd worn that same fantasy as comfort against the pain his disappearance had caused.

Armand's eyes twinkled with devilish delight, sending a swell of confusion sweeping through her. He was an old man, one of her only living relatives. He couldn't possibly want anything but her well-being, could he?

"There's no need to protect the child." For once, Armand's silken voice did nothing to smooth the goose bumps skittering up her arms. Nor did the cup of hot tea Marguerite placed before her. "Rosane is part of the legacy. In time she, too, will take her rightful place."

"Rightful place? What do you mean? What legacy?"

"All in good time."

What was happening? Why did Armand's charm suddenly make her tense? She grabbed the photo album with both hands and hugged it to her chest like armor. She couldn't have explained the feeling of abandonment that keened through her. Was she in danger? More important, was Rosane? There was no estate, no inheritance, no money other than her pitiful salary. Damn Daniel for planting doubts into her mind.

"Does it give you a thrill to scare people?" Daniel's frame filled the doorway. His shirt and pants looked slept-in and his hair finger-combed. Her heart lurched at the sight of him. Fear or love? One snowballed right into the other.

Her gaze automatically sprang to her daughter, gauging whether she or Daniel was closer to the child. Then a flush of heat brushed her cheeks at her foolishness. Daniel wouldn't hurt her. He'd promised.

"Ah, Daniel, it is a bit early for you, is it not?" A crooked smile spread over Armand's lips that somehow now seemed unnaturally red.

Daniel sat in the empty chair across from Christi. "It's never too early to deal with the devil."

Marguerite banged a frying pan onto the stove and snapped on a burner. She jerked open a drawer and with a loud rattle, extricated a whisk. From a low cupboard, she clanked a bowl.

"The devil exists only in legends, dear boy." Armand looked much too pleased with himself. He turned to her. "Have I scared you, *ma chère?*"

"Of course not." Christi shrugged, letting the album slip to her lap, and sipped her tea. She wasn't sure what she felt about anything at the moment.

"I was merely trying to enrich you with the most famous Mardi Gras legend of the area. You wanted to know of your past. That includes the bad as well as the good, no?"

"Is the legend bad?"

Marguerite dumped the metal bowl in the sink. It rattled against the sides before landing upside down over the drain.

"It is merely a tale to warn young girls there is a price to pay for dancing with the devil."

Was he trying to warn her to stay away from Daniel? Her gaze jumped from Armand to Daniel and back. Had she become the pawn again? Were they playing for her attention, the way Armand and Marguerite had vied for Rosane's? The sudden tension between the two men was palpable. Daniel's long silence didn't help matters. What was he thinking behind that intense frown?

Rosane tugged at the skirt of Christi's flannel gown and mouthed, "Who is he?"

"Daniel is a guest," Armand said, saving Christi from the fluster of her own thoughts. She needed time to sort through all this and was given none.

"Can I watch TV?" Rosane asked, cradling the kitten in her arms.

"For a few minutes. As soon as I get dressed, we're going to go shopping for some snow pants so you can play with the little girl next door."

"Okay."

Armand folded his discarded newspaper. Tucking it under his arm, he rose. "If you will excuse me, I have some business to attend to. You may keep the album. Perhaps this afternoon we can share an apéritif and I will tell you about the time your mother stole Marguerite's beau and about the hair-pulling match that followed on the church steps. Or maybe you would like to hear about the Christmas we all got the mumps."

All of it. She wanted to hear all the stories that would bring her closer to her mother. "Will you tell me why she left?"

A twinge of pain pierced his features. He suddenly

looked old and vulnerable. Not like the devil at all, but like the shadow of the healthy man he'd once been. ''If you wish.''

Daniel had to be wrong. There was no subterfuge. Whatever game existed between them had nothing to do with her. ''Thank you.''

Marguerite placed a cup of coffee and a plate of scrambled eggs and toast before Daniel, then attacked the sinkful of dishes with enough vigor to dislodge industrial slime.

Christi drained the last of her tea, but couldn't force herself to eat any more of the toast. As she moved the chair back to get up, it screeched against the linoleum tiles.

Daniel leaned forward across the table and placed a hand over her forearm. His touch, soft as sin and just as seductive, shivered all the way down to the soles of her bare feet. ''I have a meeting this morning, but don't think you can escape me. We need to settle this thing between us.''

Nestling the album in one arm, she rose, uncharacteristically unsure of what she wanted to say. ''You promised me a week.''

''Before you make your decision, not before I get you out of here.''

ARMAND SAW the pictures clearly in his mind. The colors were gone, but the contrast of black against white made his memories that much more vivid.

He was eighteen and walking back from a *soirée dansante* with his cousin Caroline and his sister Marguerite. He'd had a little too much to drink and done too little dancing to wear it off. That was the only reason he could imagine why he'd made such a monumental error.

"Ah, Armand, you were an impulsive fool then, but you have grown since and learned the value of patience. This time, you will allow no mistake."

Winter's cold bite and the wine cellar's peaceful darkness engulfed the small space, but the wine would keep him warm and he didn't need light to see the past. By the dim glow of the weak sun eking through the dirty square window, he poured himself another glass of red wine and savored half its contents before he allowed the movie in his mind to restart. He reviewed the film of that night long ago, immersed himself in the memories.

Ma belle Caroline.

"Do you know who you are?" he'd asked her as their boots crunched the hard-packed snow on the sidewalk.

"Of course I do. I'm your cousin, Caroline Rose Langelier. I'm not the one who drank too much wine tonight. You are." She'd laughed at him and hooked her arm through his.

"No, you're more than that. You're a direct descendant of Rose Latulippe."

"Did you hear that, Marguerite?" Caroline called back to her cousin trailing behind them. "I'm a descendant of a lost soul." Then she teased him with a playful tickle. "Maybe you're right, Armand. I danced with a lot of devils tonight!"

"You don't understand." Armand stopped and grabbed her arms as he faced her. "You're special." The intensity of his belief must have frightened her for he saw the color drain from her cheeks.

"Armand, are you all right?"

"Yes, yes. Don't you see? With your soul, I could buy eternal life." He'd seen it so clearly then—her still beating heart in his hands, her last breath trapped in his mouth, his body tingling with the reward of never-ending life.

Her amusement tinkled ice-clear in the dark night. "I think we better get you home and in bed."

When he squeezed her arms too tight, her laughter died and her eyes rounded in fright.

"Marguerite?" she pleaded to his sister, but her frightened gaze remained locked with his.

Impatient, as usual, Marguerite wrenched his death grip from Caroline's arms. "Armand, stop it! Can't you see you're scaring her?" She walked between them the rest of the way home.

Armand drained the remainder of his glass of wine and poured himself another.

He'd wasted years trying to find Caroline after she ran away. Her choice of a military life married to a foreigner was a good one. The frequent moves had made her hard to trace. She must have panicked when she realized Fort Worth was their last stop before her husband's retirement.

Christiane was eighteen by the time he found them again. Except for the lighter shade of hair, she was the spitting image of her mother at that age. But he'd sent a boy to do a man's job and lost another nine years waiting for his prize.

Now his human body had betrayed him. He could wait no longer. He'd had to engineer Caro's death. Only then could he lure Christiane home where she belonged.

Lifting his glass in a toast, he saluted the darkness. "To you, Caro. And to the gift of your daughter. I'm sure you understand why her presence here is necessary. I have so little time left."

Chapter Four

Christi sped through her morning routine, eager to get out of the house and away from the venomlike antagonism writhing between Daniel and Armand and poisoning the atmosphere. She and Rosane were on their way to the Galeries de la Capitale via the city bus.

As the bus bounced along Grande-Allée and the house disappeared from view, her spirits lifted. The sun sparkled against the snowbanks and warmed her heart, if not the air. She'd purposefully donned her brightest red sweater over her favorite black pants and her wild parrot earrings to cheer her. Now, she found she didn't need the external props. She was just another mother going to enjoy a day of shopping with her daughter. Tomorrow was soon enough for a serious discussion, she decided, and shrugged off the pinprick of guilt.

The Galeries de la Capitale was a huge two-level mall that boasted more than two hundred and fifty stores, boutiques and restaurants. Large glass windows ran the length of the ceiling down the center courtyard, giving the place a light and airy feel.

"Look, Mom!" Rosane pointed toward the Mega-Parc at the lone skater on the rink. A girl glided easily over the smooth surface as her coach shouted instructions. "Can I try that?"

"It's harder than it looks, honey." Christi laughed, remembering the many times she'd wished for a padded bottom when she'd learned to skate.

"Can I? Pe-lease?"

Christi couldn't refuse Rosane anything when she put on her pleading face. "Let's go shopping first."

They saw familiar names like Sears and The Gap among the sea of unfamiliar ones. At La Baie, they found a sale on everything they needed and left the store with two big shopping bags crammed full.

On impulse, Christi ducked into a music store. Music reflected its author. Maybe she could get an insight on what had changed Daniel through his work. She chose a CD of his first album, *Shifting Sands,* released five years ago and a CD of his latest album, *Âme d'Hiver,* winter's soul, released for the Christmas shopping season. She fingered the single red rose on a bed of crystallized snow. To the CDs, she added an inexpensive player and a pack of batteries.

She and Rosane browsed several boutiques before they reached a bookstore.

"How come they have a library in a mall?" Rosane asked.

"*Librairie* is French for bookstore, honey."

"Can I pick out a couple of books? I've read the one I brought already."

"Sure."

Christi wandered the aisles until she reached the mythology section and started leafing through books.

"Can I go find my books now?" Rosane asked, fidgeting.

"Sure. Just stay where I can see you." Christi's

fingers eagerly snatched several books from the shelf. She'd found the titles she wanted. What answers would they give her?

Unconsciously, her hand dropped to her coat pocket and searched for the roll of Tums she kept there. As she read on, she didn't even notice the minty chalk sliding down her throat.

NEAR QUEBEC CITY, 1698. Mardi Gras.

Outside a tempest of the devil's own making brewed. Winds howled. Snow swirled. Temperatures chilled bones to the marrow. But inside, a fire roared and laughter rang loud and warm on this February night.

This was the grandest party of the decade. The whole village was here, feasting and drinking on her father's generous provisions. Paul, her fiancé, stood at her elbow, his adoration plain on his face. To be sixteen, in love and the center of attention was glorious. Rose had never been happier.

When the music started, she could not keep her feet still and tapped them in rhythm to the fiddler's lively beat and to the piano's spirited song. Paul didn't care much for dancing, so she took turns waltzing and spinning with every man in the room. With every twirl on the floor, energy sang through her limbs and her whole body tingled with excitement.

Late in the evening, during a breather between songs, someone blustered in. A tall stranger stood in the doorway, his coat white with snow, his beard crystalled with frost.

"I've lost my way in the storm," he said. "May I rest for a while?"

"Of course," her father answered, ushering the stranger in. "On this night, even the dogs come in."

The stranger removed his fur-lined coat. Rose gasped at the sight of him. Clothed in velvet, silk and lace, he was the finest man she'd ever seen.

"Your hat and gloves, *monsieur?*" her father asked, eyeing the rich accessories.

"I'm still cold. Perhaps after I warm up a little by your fire."

"Of course, of course. Make yourself at home."

The stranger smiled brightly. Rose's heart fluttered at the beauty of it. He was the most handsome man in New France.

"I apologize for disturbing your party." To Rose, his voice sounded like warmed honey and it trickled through her deliciously.

"Nonsense," her father said. "The more, the merrier."

"Please carry on and ignore me."

Rose's brother glanced out the window at the storm. "By all that's holy! That's quite a horse you've got there."

People crowded in twos and threes around the small windows to take a look. There, all black and sleek, stood the most magnificent horse they'd ever seen. Despite the storm whirling around him, not a speck of snow stuck to the animal's lustrous coat.

Her brother almost panted with his eagerness to get his hands on such a fine steed. "Shall I stable him for you?"

"That won't be necessary. I'll be on my way shortly."

Réal, the fiddler, took up his bow. Ti-Jean poised

his hands above the piano keys. And the music started once more.

"May I join the dance?" the stranger asked Rose's father.

"Most assuredly." Her father handed him a glass of spirits.

The stranger downed the liquor, thanked her father and strode toward her. Heat seared her cheeks and a zing of delight coursed through her.

"*Mademoiselle,* would you give me the pleasure of the next dance?"

"Why, of course, *monsieur.*" Did she sound as breathless as she felt? Shyly, she stepped into the circle of his arms and waited for him to lead her onto the floor.

He danced with grace and elegance. Rose found it hard to tear her gaze from his beautiful face—the dark eyes, the fine bones, the smile that suggested sensuous secrets. She danced, once, twice and yet another time with him. He was the only man in the room who hadn't stepped on her toes as he twirled her about. In his arms, she was light, beautiful and entirely feminine. If only this evening could go on forever!

Rose spotted Paul pouting on the sidelines. He scowled and threw her heated daggers every time their gazes connected. But she didn't care. When would she get another chance to dance with someone so sophisticated? She and Paul would share the rest of their lives together. This stranger would leave soon.

The first stroke of midnight sounded in the middle of a lively measure. A collective groan rippled through the room. Dancers slowed. The piano music faded.

Her father rose from his chair. "Thank you, Réal, Ti-Jean. Thank you everyone for coming to Rose's Mardi Gras party. It is now Ash Wednesday and the celebration must stop."

Rose moved to disengage herself from the stranger's arms, but he held her firm. "Let's finish this song."

"We can't. It's—"

"We must."

Rose tried to still her feet, but they kept moving as if they had a will of their own. The sound of the clock on the mantel chiming each stroke of the midnight hour pealed like doom through the room.

"Réal!" her father shouted. "The music must stop. Now!"

"I can't! The bow, it's moving on its own. I can't stop my fingers!"

Everyone else had ceased dancing. They stood around the wheeling couple and buzzed their disapproval. Rose's heart beat faster than the music. She caught Paul's gaze as she and the stranger spun near him. *Help me!*

All at once, the stranger drew her hard against him. He bent his head and whispered in her ear. "You are mine. I will take you for my bride."

Before Rose could voice her protest, something sharp pricked her palm. Pain and panic charged through her faster than a runaway carriage. Her feet came off the ground. Her body became weightless and tingly. Her cry of despair made no sound.

Faster and faster the stranger reeled her around the floor. The room spun until everything became a blur. Smoke rose from the stranger's feet, engulfing them.

She could no longer feel her body.

"Mine," the stranger said. "Forever."

The stranger's beautiful face bent closer to hers. His fetid breath poured into her. As he deepened his kiss, her heat, her life, her soul seeped out. Her body slumped, limp and lifeless. And even as her eyes closed for the last time, on the darkness of her lids, she could still see the devil's smile of satisfaction.

CHRISTI PUT the latest book back on the shelf with a sigh. Some versions of the legend claimed Rose survived her brush with the devil, but was never the same. She remained a spinster and never laughed or attended a party again. Other versions said she married her fiancé, but bore him no children. Still others claimed that once the parish priest had saved her from the devil's grasp, she never uttered another word and spent the rest of her life rocking herself, staring at the world through blank eyes.

Well, how cheerful. Christi couldn't see what any of this had to do with her or what part of the legend she was supposed to fulfill. What could possibly hold so much significance in Armand's mind?

Rosane tugged at Christi's coat sleeve. "Mom, can I have this book?"

Christi glanced distractedly at the book. "You can't read French."

"I know, but you could read it to me. I want to learn."

Christi crouched so she could meet Rosane at eye level. "I think it's better if Armand and Marguerite don't know I speak French."

"Why?"

Christi sighed. How could she explain to an eight-year-old a reluctance she herself didn't understand?

This was all Daniel's fault. If he hadn't colored her impressions with doubt, she wouldn't be twitching at every shadow—like her mother had for all of her life. "I'm not very good at speaking it, and I don't want to have to try to carry on a conversation."

"Why?"

"Because." She didn't like resorting to "because." She'd always hated it when her mother had done the same thing. "It'll be our secret, okay?"

Rosane shrugged indifferently. She held up two young adult mysteries. "Can I have these then?"

"Sure." One disaster averted. How many more to go? Christi chose several of the legend books and added them to Rosane's stack. She wanted more time to study the nuances of the legend at home. While she paid for their selections, Rosane tugged on her sleeve again. "Can we go skating now?"

"Do you want some lunch first?" Christi accepted the package from the clerk and stuffed it into the larger of her shopping bags.

"Uh-uh. I wanna play."

"All right." Playing sounded good. Legends and devils and lovers back from the dead could wait another couple of hours to haunt her again.

DANIEL SPOTTED them as they left the bookstore. Two blobs of color against the neutral background. Christiane's bright red sweater was a beacon against her white stadium-length coat. Rosane was a bouncing fuchsia ball next to her mother. He followed them to the rental booth near the skating rink and watched them stow away their purchases in a locker. In the background, the tinny music of the nearby carousel grated against his ear.

Rosane squirmed as Christiane tightened the laces on the boots of her skates. "Do you think Fumée misses me?"

"I'm sure she does. And I'm sure Marguerite is taking good care of her."

"How long did it take you to learn to skate?"

"Oh, I don't remember. It was a long time ago. In Germany when your grandfather was stationed there." She tweaked her daughter's nose, and her songbird laugh struck a chord deep in his gut. "I fell a lot."

Rosane pushed Christiane's hand away and stood unsteadily. "Show me."

Christiane took a few tentative strokes on the ice. She soon remembered how to balance and grew bolder with each glide. She skated back to Rosane, then skated backwards, pulling Rosane along so the girl could get the feel of the ice. More than once they ended up flat on their bottoms, Christiane laughing like the teenager Daniel remembered and Rosane dusting herself off seriously, not quite able to hide her smile of pleasure.

Daniel longed to join them. Under normal circumstances, he'd be a part of their family. Now he was the enemy. He'd recognized his new status in Christiane's manner at breakfast. A civil, restrained demeanor that added no warmth to the cold house. Having been cast in the role of villain chipped at his soul, but it was his rightful place.

His daughter was a total stranger. Except for one picture of her as a baby, this morning was the first time he'd seen his child. She'd been quiet. Her big gray eyes—Christiane's eyes—assessed him frankly. And all he'd done was stare back. *Hello, I'm your long-lost father* would certainly have shocked her and gained him Christiane's wrath.

In Rosane's movements, as her gangly limbs tried to reach a compromise with the ice, he saw himself. Hadn't he been her age when he'd first found his father in a compromising position? Regret seeped through his carefully erected wall. He didn't want to destroy her world the way his father had destroyed his. He would protect her—no matter what the cost.

He'd missed everything, from her first cry to her first step. And he'd miss everything to come—her graduation, her first date, her wedding—if he couldn't convince Christiane to marry him. A wave of sadness sank through him. Before he could judge the wisdom of his impulse, he rented a pair of skates.

As he opened the entry panel to the rink, his hands gripped the wood tightly. He skated toward the duo, who had once more fallen in a heap on the ice. He easily skirted two boys passing a hockey puck and stopped beside Christiane and Rosane with a flurry of ice crystals.

"What are you doing here?" Christiane's voice was colder than the ice, but he let it slide over him.

"Helping two very beautiful ladies to their feet." That his smile disconcerted her pleased him. Keeping her off balance would crack her defenses.

She jerked her hand from his grasp. "I don't need your help, thank you. What are you really doing here?"

She did have a talent for getting straight to the heart of things. "You've had a lifetime. Let me have an hour."

A zap of fear flashed through her eyes. Her mouth dropped open in silent panic. "You agreed."

"I just want a few moments." The cadence of his fast-beating heart filled the heavy pause. "How can I make you believe if you won't give me a chance?" Pleading didn't come easily. "Trust me, Christiane."

Remembrance, fear, indecision all paraded wildly through her expressive eyes. Could she understand his curiosity to know his own flesh and blood? Or did she see him only as the monster who could take away her child? He wouldn't, couldn't, but why should she believe him? "Please."

"Mom?"

At the plaintive cry, they both turned to the object of their debate.

"It's all right, honey." Christiane struggled to stand and helped Rosane up. "We're leaving now."

Rosane stopped dusting the frost from her jeans. "But Mom, I was just getting it."

Daniel seized on the opportunity Rosane handed him. "And you're doing quite well, too. Would you like me to teach you more? I play hockey with friends most Wednesday nights, so you know I'm a good skater."

"Do you know how to twirl and jump?" Rosane mimicked the desired moves with her fingers.

"Of course."

Eyes bright with anticipation, Rosane whipped her head toward her mother. "Pe-lease?"

Christiane glared at him. Red-faced and fists clenched in tight balls at her sides, she couldn't allow her temper to explode. Causing a scene had always distressed her. And causing a scene here would mean explanations he was sure she didn't want to get into in public.

A hockey puck came flying past his head, missing

him by less than an inch. Instantly, her fists unknotted. Her face paled. Her lower lip trembled. He spun
on his blades, becoming her shield against the next
missile.

"Sorry," one of the boys said, pointing sheepishly
at the black disk at Daniel's feet. "It got away from
me."

Daniel picked up the puck and tossed it to the boy.
"Be more careful next time."

As he skated back toward her, Christiane hunched
her shoulders as if they were wings protecting her
heart. "Fifteen minutes."

His heart knocked hard as Rosane bounced in
place. His throat too thick to speak, he nodded at
Christiane.

Now that he could touch his daughter, a certain
reluctance scratched his palms. How would a normal
father act with his daughter? He had no idea and the
magnitude of the task rendered him speechless.

You've taught dozens of kids how to skate. She's
just one more. But she wasn't one of Sister Marie-
Ange's orphans. She was his own child. He wanted,
no needed, to get it right.

Rosane looked up at him expectantly. "What do I
do first?"

His fear vanished. Everything would be all right.
She wanted to learn and had accepted him as a
teacher. That was enough for now. He took her
gloved hand in his and cherished its delicate weight.
Then he flashed her his biggest smile. "First, you
separate your feet. Like so. Do you know how to ride
a bike?"

"Yes, but only in the park. Mom won't let me ride
in the street."

''That's very wise of her. Skating is like riding a bike. It's a different way to balance. First the weight is on one side. Like this. Then on the other. Like that.''

Rosane copied his every move and pride swelled his heart. He glanced at Christiane's form huddled against the boards and silently thanked her.

For the first time in his life, he understood the magnitude of the price he'd paid for choosing to leave.

DANIEL'S LOOK sent a shiver of recognition tingling through Christi's body. In that instant, he was the Daniel she remembered—the rugged face, the warm smile and the unruly passion that had so moved her. The memory tugged on her heartstrings, connecting them for a moment. She could almost hear him wish for things to have worked out differently.

Ridiculous. A figment of her imagination. She was too good at rewriting the parts of her life she didn't like. If she kept this up, she'd end up in a padded cell.

They looked good together, father and daughter. Daniel wore faded jeans that accentuated the long, lean lines of his body and a fisherman's sweater under his black ski jacket. And his patience with Rosane made her want to believe in a happy ending for them all.

Tears pressured the corners of her eyes. Holding them back, she shook her head. Wishes were for little girls, and as Daniel had pointed out last night, they were both grown-ups. She popped two Tums into her mouth and crunched them as she leaned against the boards.

She'd often wondered what would happen if they

ever met again, but had never thought it would happen. Now all she could do was worry. Rosane was an innocent victim, and Christi wanted to shelter her from the pain of the truth. Would Rosane notice her own slight resemblance to Daniel? Would her sensitive daughter feel their tie? How best to tell her about him?

Enough now, stomach. I don't think our insurance covers medical treatment in a foreign country.

Daniel was a good teacher and Rosane learned fast. She was soon zipping across the ice with competent strokes, turning and even trying her hand at skating backwards. When she started to show signs of fatigue, Daniel gently led her back to the boards where Christi waited.

"Well, you look like a real skater now." Christi hugged her daughter close, staking her claim to the child.

"Did you see me stop?" Rosane asked breathlessly.

"I sure did. That was great."

"Can we come again? Daniel still has to teach me to twirl and jump."

"We'll see."

"Tomorrow?"

"We'll see."

Rosane pouted. "That always means no."

Christi smiled, but unease tightened her stomach into a determined fist. Reality seemed to unravel and reinvent itself with each passing moment. What had she done? Why had she let Daniel close to Rosane? How could she not have predicted a new network of bonds would form? "It means we'll see."

Rosane chatted endlessly about what she'd learned

as they removed their skates and retrieved their packages. Daniel wisely remained on the edge of their orbit.

"I'll drive you home," he said when Christi took Rosane's hand and started heading toward the bus stop.

"No, that's all right. We'll take the bus."

"With all those packages?"

She fished through her pocket and waved two tickets. "I've already paid the fare."

"I have a trunk for all those bags, comfortable seats and a heater that works."

Christi tightened her hold on Rosane's hand and pushed toward the exit. "We'd rather take the bus."

"Christiane…" The catch in his voice tore at her.

"Don't. Please don't."

"Where's the harm?"

"You promised."

Rosane glanced at Daniel, then gave her a pleading appeal. "Mom, I'm hungry."

Daniel shoved his hands in his pockets as if it were the only way to prevent them from reaching out and keeping her here. "At least let me buy you both some lunch."

Then he glanced at Rosane and her heart bled. No, this wasn't happening. He wasn't falling in love with his own daughter. He couldn't.

"Mo-o-om," Rosane whined. "I'm hun-gry."

This was her fault. She should have insisted Rosane eat before skating. She should have been stronger and not allowed Daniel the time he'd wanted. Now she was having to deal with the consequences of her mistakes.

"All right." She speared Daniel's amber eyes to

make sure he would get the full meaning of her capitulation. *You win. This time.*

"Thank you," he whispered as he led them toward the food court.

As Rosane made her selection, Christi cast a furtive glance in Daniel's direction. His profile was relaxed. His sensual mouth curved into a half smile that softened the hard planes of his cheekbones. His gaze feasted on his daughter as if he were trying to cram nine years into the minutes she'd allotted him.

A flicker of memory startled her. He'd looked soft like this when he'd enticed her to claim sickness and cut her shift at the ice-cream parlor short. She could see him in her mind's eye looking at her and smiling secretly this way as he stood right by the shop's door, waiting.

She swallowed the memory and felt it land with a thud in the pit of her stomach. With the heel of her hand, she broke it apart. Snapping her gaze away, she tried to concentrate on finding an empty table.

They'd both changed. She had to remember that. They shared a daughter. It was too late to pretend he was still dead. But that didn't mean there was any future for them.

One of the packages slipped when she put it on a seat. As she caught it, the other one tumbled to the ground, spilling its contents. A book of legends gashed through its bag.

Talking nonstop about skating, Rosane sat while Daniel pushed the tray of food onto the table. "Let me."

He bent down to retrieve the book just as Christi reached for it. He stared at the cover for a moment, then at her. "Armand did scare you."

She snatched the book from his hand and stuffed it into the big bag. "Of course not. I just wanted to read the legend, that's all."

He reached for the two coffees on the tray and handed her a take-out cup. "Did you read it?"

"Yes, but I don't see why Armand is so obsessed with it." She twirled the hot cup of coffee around and around.

"Obsession has no logic. That's what makes it so dangerous."

Christi cocked her head. "Speaking from personal experience?"

His eyes shadowed as if a ghost were haunting them. "Experience, yes."

"You know what your problem is?" Christi plucked a fry from Rosane's tray. Her tired daughter didn't protest the theft. "Your problem is that you expect everyone to open themselves to you, but you want the right to stay all closed up. You want trust. But trust has to work both ways."

He glanced at Rosane whose eyes were at half-mast as she slowly chewed on her burger. His regret echoed inside Christi.

"If I'd known where you were," she whispered, "I would have told you."

Daniel nodded. A knot of emotion seemed to slide down his throat. He reached for her hand and squeezed it tight. "Be careful, Christiane. Not everything is as it seems."

Chapter Five

Christi waited for Daniel and Armand's voices to fade from the kitchen before she came down for breakfast the next morning. After her restless night of sleep, she was in no mood to face either of them. She'd dreamed of demons bending over her, of icy blankets and searing kisses, and had woken up with a jackhammer headache scoring through the soft tissues beneath her skull.

Without a word, Marguerite placed a cup of mint tea, two slices of toast and a soft-boiled egg before her. Christi thanked her and Marguerite harrumphed. As she opened one of the books of Canadian legends she'd bought yesterday, the pages rippled to the legend of Rose Latulippe.

Minutes later, the prickly spine feeling of being watched had her glancing up to find Marguerite's magnified eyes peering curiously at her from across the table.

"It will not help you," Marguerite said in her painful English. She sipped from her steaming mug of coffee.

"Pardon me?"

"The book." Marguerite nodded toward the volume Christi read.

"I'm sorry. I don't understand."

"Armand, he make his own legend. He believe Rose can save him."

Christi shut the book and pressed her hands on the cover. "How can she when she's not real?"

Marguerite's gaze hovered somewhere above her head as if she could somehow capture the words she sought from the air. "He study *généalogie*. He discover Rose have a child—a girl."

"None of the legends I've read mention any children."

Marguerite leaned forward as if she were imparting a secret. "It was the devil's child."

Considering how Rose and the devil spent their time together, the fact appeared improbable, but Marguerite seemed convinced she spoke the truth. Or was she just trying to scare her? Despite Marguerite's courteous manners, Christi had sensed the older woman's dislike from their first meeting. Time hadn't lessened the impression. "It's a legend, Marguerite. Fiction."

"Your *grand-maman,* Catherine. She was the ten generation. Your *maman,* Caroline, she was the eleven. You are the twelve. Rosane is the thirteen."

"Descendants of Rose Latulippe?" Christi asked, barely able to mask her incredulity. Where was Marguerite heading with all of this?

"Always only one daughter for thirteen generations." Marguerite's satisfied smile left Christi feeling as if she'd been slapped with an ice-cold hand. Was Daniel right? Had Armand twisted some old legend to suit some personal agenda? If so, how did this generational delusion affect her? Did he think she could take Rose's place?

"Marguerite, even if that were true, what does that mean to Armand? And how does Daniel fit in with all of this?"

"Armand used Daniel. He promised him that his mother and sister would not have to suffer any more. Daniel he believed, but—" As if Marguerite realized she'd said too much, a speck of fear flashed through her huge black eyes. Her lips rolled inward as if she were trying to suck her words back in. She heaved herself off the chair. "You must ask Armand."

Christi reached for Marguerite's sleeve, stopping her flight. "Why won't you tell me?"

"It is not my business." Marguerite's jerky arm movement, as she released her sleeve from Christi's clutch, sloshed coffee over the rim of her cup and stained the front of her starched white apron.

"But it involves me, doesn't it? Don't I have a right to know?"

Marguerite whisked away the remnants of Christi's half-eaten breakfast and headed for the sink. "You must ask Armand."

Her tone of finality and the rush of water prevented any further conversation. Maybe Daniel was wrong and it was Marguerite whose brain matter wasn't quite arranged right.

Christi drummed her fingers against the tabletop. She'd spent yesterday evening listening to Daniel's CDs only to realize she didn't know enough about music to make the analysis she'd wanted.

Daniel's music was sensual, angry, unforgettable. Both CDs were replete with haunting beauty—and caution. Both had taken her on a roller-coaster ride of memories and emotions, and sowed questions like wind through a dandelion field. Neither had given her a solid clue to the man whose fingers could wreak such magic on her skin, or answers as to what demons caged his soul.

She turned her attention back to the book with its colorful drawings of a young girl with brown hair and blue eyes being twirled around the floor by a charming devil in fine clothes. Armand seemed obsessed with the legend and Daniel with protecting her from Armand's obsession.

Her father was a great believer in discipline and strategy. A good general, he'd say, knows his opposition. She needed to park her emotional response to all that was happening around her and come up with a definite plan. If Daniel was right and Armand had evil intentions toward her, then something, somewhere in this house would give him away.

"How long will Armand be out?" Christi asked Marguerite, the niggling of an idea forming. Not the greatest of plans, but it was a start.

Marguerite snapped shut the water, dried her hands and slipped on yellow rubber gloves. "I do not know. He go with Daniel to the *théâtre.*"

"Oh."

"He will not miss lunch."

"Thank you. I'll ask him about the legend then."

Marguerite shrugged and turned her attention to the dishes.

If Armand and Daniel came back for lunch, that left her with a couple of hours to see what she could find. She glanced back at Marguerite. How long would it take her to finish her task? Marguerite believed in hot meals, so she would certainly start on lunch soon. If she kept a sharp ear for Marguerite's heavy footsteps, she could do this.

She checked on Rosane. Her daughter sat sprawled in a rocking chair watching television in French with a contented Fumée purring in her lap.

Christi leaned against the door frame. "How's it going, kiddo?"

Rosane glanced up, then flicked her gaze back to the screen. "Fine. They give the cartoons funny voices. Are we going to do anything today?"

"We'll go exploring after lunch. How does that sound?"

"Can I wear my new boots?"

"You most certainly can."

"Can we go skating?"

"We'll see."

Rosane laughed at the antics of Popeye and Olive Oyl, disturbing the kitten that peered up at her with one eye. Christi left them and headed for the back of the house.

Each floorboard cackled like an old hag, announcing to the world her less-than-honest intentions. The black-and-white stripes on the wallpaper of the hallway reminded her irrationally of jail bars. Her mind heard the shadowy walls whisper dire warnings and the faceless doors dared her to unveil their secrets. With every step, her palms grew damper, her heart knocked faster and her resolve slipped a notch.

Armand's office stood at the end of the hall. The dark wood of the closed door suddenly seemed like the mouth of an ogre waiting to swallow her up. She hesitated, but finally moved forward.

Her wet palms slipped on the brass knob. It snapped loudly back into place. She listened intently for the sound of Marguerite's footsteps and heard only the slow tocking of the grandfather clock at the bottom of the stairs. She wiped her hands on the thigh of her blue corduroy pants and tried again.

She wasn't cut out for this. Always before when she'd acted, it was to make others more comfortable and to be accepted. Playing the spy was something she'd never done before. Never again, she vowed, as she dug in her pants pocket, but found them empty. No Tums.

Half-expecting Armand's thin smile to greet her, she pushed the door open. A sigh of relief escaped her when his face didn't materialize in the murky darkness of the room.

The stench of cigarette mixed with his spicy cologne assaulted her nose. The stale, unmoving air of the room enshrouded her like a mummy in a tomb. Her breakfast crept up to her throat. She swallowed it back down, along with her rising trepidations. What choice did she have? Both Armand and Daniel refused to answer her questions and she needed answers.

After a few minutes, her eyes adjusted to the near total darkness of Armand's office. A shaft of dusty sunlight thrust itself through a crack where the heavy drapes didn't quite meet. On the wall, the narrow band of light cast wraithlike shadows whose icy fingers skimmed her chilled skin.

Don't be ridiculous. It's just the cold air, not the shadows.

She wrapped her arms beneath her chest and rubbed them to keep the glacial atmosphere from penetrating her skull. Hands out in front of her, she patted her way to the drapes and pushed them open a few more inches.

Armand's office offered a barren landscape of black on black with few touches of light or life to add a respite. Only one single framed diploma graced the wall behind the desk. A Chinese mountain scene done in marquetry decorated the ebony lacquer armoire on the back wall. In the pale light, the dull gold fringe surrounding the raven carpet shone like emergency floor lights in a theater. The whole room struck her as out of character even for Armand. She'd expected a masculine den, trimmed with leather and comfort, not this minimalist Asian decor.

On the plain black desk, she spotted a small photograph. "Oh," she said when she realized it was of her mother at eighteen. With shaky fingers, she picked it up.

Caroline was beautiful. Short brown hair curled around her face. She wore large pearl earrings clipped to her ears and a pearl necklace around her neck. A sweet, innocent smile graced her lips. Her smooth skin showed none of the deeply etched lines of worry Christi was so familiar with. A veil of sadness draped over Christi's shoulders. She'd never known this happy side of her mother.

She replaced the picture, making sure she repositioned the frame exactly as she'd found it. She riffled through the drawers, careful not to disturb the meticulous lie of Armand's possessions.

The black file cabinet next to the armoire was empty, except for a midnight blue velvet jeweler's box. Inside the box, draped artfully on a white satin background, lay a gold oval locket. A fancy scroll etched its face and rubies and diamonds encrusted its border. Gently she squeezed the small button on the side and the cover sprang open.

She gasped. The box dropped from her hands, leaving the pendant dangling from her icy fingers. The left half of the frame contained a picture of her at nineteen. The right half held a picture of Rosane taken one month after her birth.

Her fingers shook as she reached to touch the photographs. How had Armand gotten those pictures? It didn't make sense. She hadn't even known the Langeliers existed until a month ago. But Armand had known exactly where she was for these past nine years. Why wait so long to make his presence known? Why wait until her parents were dead? Was that it? Her mother wouldn't have allowed the reunion, and Armand knew that? Why? Always why? The damned question had dogged her all of her life, and everyone seemed intent on refusing to answer it.

Absently, she closed the locket and rubbed the gold scroll with a thumb. "Daniel, what's going on here and why won't you tell me?"

When the answer failed to materialize, she returned the locket to its velvet box and the box to the depths of the file cabinet drawer.

Nothing here indicated anything about Rose Latulippe or Armand's research on genealogy. He must keep it elsewhere. Did he still practice law and rent an office? She'd have to find out without arousing his suspicions.

"And then what? Are you going to snoop there, too?" Why not, if that was the only way to get answers?

A board creaked on the stairway and two male

voices, arguing, floated toward her. Great. How would she explain her presence here?

She raced for the door, cracked it open. Armand and Daniel had reached the last curve of the stairs and would easily spot her if she tried to leave. A rush of panic swarmed over her.

"Think! Come on, *think!*"

Pacing from door to desk and back, she saw no connecting door, no balcony, no screen to hide her. The chair provided a pitiful armor. The desk displayed straight black legs and open space. The drapes didn't reach the floor.

Think! Think!

The steps paused outside the door. She stopped her aimless pacing.

Just as the knob twisted, she dove into the armoire.

CHRISTI WAS SURE they could hear the wild hammering of her heart, then realized they were too engrossed in their argument to notice that or the soft clicking of the armoire door shutting behind her on her way to safety. Slowly, she uncurled her fisted fingers, forced her shoulders to relax and her breath to quiet.

"You know I am a patron of the arts," Armand said in French. "They simply asked for my opinion."

"I don't care. I don't want you there," Daniel shot back, his voice harsh with barely controlled rage.

"My presence is no concern of yours."

The curtains, being drawn farther apart, snapped, startling her. She inhaled her gasp and calmed her racing pulse with a soothing count of breath. In, one, two, three, four. Hold, one two, three, four. Out, one, two, three, four.

"What's the real reason?" Daniel asked. "It can't

be for your expertise. Did you buy your way on the committee?''

Buy his way? Daniel's tone of voice left her with the impression he'd done it before.

As Armand's body sank into the creaky swivel chair behind his desk, Christi flattened her face against the door to peer out of the keyhole. The slashes of light accented the bony structure of Armand's face, giving it a skeletal look. ''You're acting like a spoiled brat. It doesn't become you. If your fans knew, you would lose their respect.''

''I'm not worried about their opinions, but I am worried about your plans for Christiane.''

''Plans. What plans? The arts committee asked you to compose a new piece for them for the Mardi Gras celebration. They sent three directors to listen to the preview. It was a coincidence that I was chosen. And, as it happens, we are all in agreement that the piece you performed was not what we contracted you for. I've already explained all this to you. You are much too cynical.''

''With good reason.'' She couldn't see Daniel, but could feel the piercing tip of his glare directed right between Armand's eyes. ''Are you planning on finishing what you started with Christiane's mother? What would killing her gain you?''

Armand reached into his jacket and took out a cigarette case and a lighter. The strike of his lighter coming to flame charged the silence with fiery expectation. ''What's this outburst really about, Daniel?''

''You gave me your word.'' Daniel ground the words out, spitting them out as if they were bitter. ''You said that if I never got in touch with her, you would leave her alone.''

With a hand on her mouth, Christi trapped her gasp of surprise. Armand and Daniel had struck a bargain for her life? Why?

Armand puffed on his cigarette, sucking in his thin cheeks and exhaled. "Circumstances have changed."

"It doesn't excuse—"

"I'm dying. Did you know that?" He held the lighted cigarette straight up by two fingers—the cause of his death sentence? She could almost hear the crackle of his paper skin as he smiled. "I need Christiane."

Christi's breath hitched and lodged high in her lungs. What for?

Daniel echoed her thought. "What for?"

"You wouldn't begrudge an old man the pleasure of knowing his family, would you?"

"Family," Daniel scoffed. "I don't believe you. I saw Caroline's scar."

Scar? What scar? She'd never seen a scar on her mother.

As Armand nodded, his stiff hair brushed his collar. "I'm an old man. I'm dying. I want to make things right. You take things much too personally."

"I take promises personally. I take your intentions toward Christiane personally. And I take my music personally. You took them both away from me once. I won't let you do it again." Daniel's voice was raw, emotions rippling thick and dark so close to the surface that, for a second, Christi feared he would unleash his anger at Armand. What had happened? What had Armand done to him, to her mother? What was happening still?

"When you take a commission," Armand said

evenly as he stubbed out his cigarette in an ashtray, "you must satisfy your client's desires."

"Not if it violates my beliefs."

"Yes! Even if it does. It's an agreement. It must be honored."

"That's immoral."

"Prostitution is an ancient concept." Armand's suit jacket rustled as he shrugged. "That's what you were paid for. You accepted the payment. You must deliver."

"I resign. The committee will have my check in the morning."

Christi couldn't see Daniel from her position in the armoire, but she could sense the lines of his body becoming rigid as his voice became more guarded.

"You have a contract with the arts committee." Armand spoke with cool indifference. "You have a contract with Amicus Records and therefore with me. You must honor them or you will definitely lose everything again."

"You're Amicus?"

"I own your career, Daniel. I own *you*."

An oppressive pause suffocated time. Neither man moved. Each of their breaths rasped the air. The bristle of sleeves as they crossed their arms slashed like scythes through dry grass. Their mutual distrust reeked of sulfur. Her lungs burned with paralysis as she waited for their thunder to rend the room.

"Now that you've seen your daughter, do you regret the past?"

As if kicked, Christi's gut recognized her desperate need to hear Daniel's answer. Uninvited, anxiety kicked in. Her heart jumped like a caged cricket. Her sweat-slicked fingers pressed against the tight dread banding her chest. Blood trooped past her ears in a mad rush. *Breathe, breathe, breathe,* she silently chanted.

The crushing silence in the room weighed as heavily as an ocean. Still neither spoke. Her nose itched from the dust she inhaled off the armoire's contents. Her chest cramped with repressed sobs. Her shaking fingers gripped the wool of the sweater over her aching heart.

"The only thing I regret is having trusted you." The icy tones of Daniel's voice made her shiver. How could a man so passionate have become so cold?

"I've treated you like a son."

"Don't *ever* call me that." Each word strained through clenched teeth. "One bastard father was enough."

"I've opened doors for you—"

"And destroyed dreams. Not just for me, but for everyone I've ever cared for." Pure hatred flowed from Daniel. Not cold at all. The passion was still there, trapped inside, ready to explode.

The chair squeaked as Armand moved closer to the desk. A drawer opened, cassettes shuffled, their plastic boxes clicking together like rat claws scrabbling on tiles.

"What happened in the past has nothing to do with this consultation for the arts committee. So calm yourself, do your job, and leave me to mine. You won't be able to escape your destiny any more than she will." He tossed a cassette to Daniel.

Daniel deftly caught it. "What's that supposed to mean?"

"Like father, like son."

Christi felt the deliberate blow impact on her solar plexus.

"I'm *nothing* like him." He clapped the cassette on top of the desk.

"Really?"

"I don't cheat. I don't lie. I protect what's mine." Daniel's steps pounded across the room. The office door slammed.

She let out her breath in a slow, quiet stream. Armand moved about the room at a restless pace. He stopped at the desk and picked up Caroline's picture.

"Why did you have to leave, Caro? See the complications you have created."

He scraped open the smallest drawer on his desk. Through the keyhole, Christi saw him pry at a panel with a letter opener. But her limited view didn't allow a clear shot at the object he pocketed.

A tentative knock rapped on the door and Rosane's tiny voice asked if she could come in. Armand closed the desk drawer and said, "Of course, *p'tit ange.*"

"Have you seen my mom?"

The tremor in Rosane's voice wrenched Christi's heart. *I'm here, baby.*

"Have you looked in her room?"

"She's not there. I've looked everywhere."

Oh, Rosie. I'll be right there.

"Perhaps she went for a walk."

"N-no, her coat is still in the closet."

"I see. I am sure she is somewhere close. We will find her. Let us go see if she did not beat us to lunch."

After the office door closed, the unmistakable sound of a key tumbling a lock into place cracked through the room like a whip.

She scrambled out of her hiding place and dusted

herself off. One look at the lock told her she could get out, but wouldn't be able to relock the door without a key. In desperation, she went to the desk and searched. All she found were a half dozen cassettes piled on top of a torn blueprint and the usual assortment of paper clips, pens and pencils. Even the space beneath the secret panel was empty. No key.

She inched the door open and peered into the hallway. Empty. She'd have to be careful. The unlocked door would warn Armand. That would place him on the defensive and that could change the direction of this awful game.

One thing was clear. Armand was the cause of her mother's perpetual fear. How or why, she wasn't sure. But he'd done something to her that had set her on a lifelong flight. Christi wasn't going to submit Rosane to the same unexplained shadow dodging her all of her life or to the endless parade of unanswered whys. She wasn't going to run. She was going to stay and face her fear.

ARMAND POCKETED the key and patted the material of the jacket. Rosane slipped her hand into his hand as they headed down the corridor, bringing a smile to his lips.

Christiane was in his office. Of this he was sure. The curtains were agape. Caroline's picture was askew. And the drawers of his desk were opened. A less observant man wouldn't have noticed the small changes, but he took heed of everything. Marguerite knew better than to invade his privacy. Daniel was with him all morning. The child would have no interest and had shown the good manners to knock and ask permission before entering private space. But her mother, ah, she presented a different story.

How much had she understood of his conversation with Daniel? How much had she understood of the things she'd seen?

Unexpected complications. He shook his head. He didn't need difficulties this close to his goal. If he didn't find a way to divert Christiane's attention, he'd have to set up surveillance again. He had too many details to oversee to waste his time in such a rudimentary fashion.

At least she hadn't found the magic. He patted his pocket, reassured by the hard contours of the small, round box.

He would have to be more careful in the future. He'd underestimated Daniel's need to protect her even above his career. He'd underestimated the depth of her need to understand her past. And he'd mistaken the direction their reunion would take. There was a strength, a power to their relationship that could ruin everything.

He couldn't have them fight their destiny the way Caroline had. Looking down at the child next to him, he realized that Christiane needed something to worry about.

Daniel would have to be dealt with, too, and that he could achieve with one phone call.

Armand smiled sweetly at the child holding his hand. Patience required time, and he was fast running out of it. A mother would sacrifice anything for her child, a lover for the object of his affection. And Daniel couldn't very well defend two forts at the same time.

LUNCH WAS a difficult affair, broken only by Rosane's bright monologue. Marguerite served a thick pea soup with fat slices of freshly baked bread, slathered with sweet butter.

Armand smiled at Rosane and feigned interest in the chatter. But Christi noticed the smile didn't quite reach the hard coal of his eyes. Daniel, wrapped in a cocoon of his own, seemed oblivious to what went on around him. And Marguerite, as usual, took everything in, but said nothing.

"Mom, are we still going exploring after lunch?"

"What a great idea!" Daniel said, surprising Christi with the brightness of his voice. "Fresh air would do me good. Can I join you?"

Before anyone could answer, Armand's crooked smile challenged Daniel. "Yes, let's make it a family affair."

Chapter Six

Christi dropped a fresh roll of Tums in her coat pocket. This outing was *not* a good idea. The fuse of impending disaster was lit in the kitchen, and it surely would wind its way to the keg of black powder that stood between Daniel and Armand and explode any time now. She didn't want to witness that mess.

Daniel pressed his hand against the small of her back to guide her out the front door with its ghoulish griffin's head knocker that looked as if it had glowing eyes. "Where are we going?"

"Rosane and I were going to walk through the old part of the city." Even through the thick layers of her clothes, the warmth of his hand branded her and already Christi was forgetting why including him was such a bad idea.

She turned abruptly and found herself nose-to-chin with Daniel. She lifted her gaze to meet his, then quickly dropped it, only to find her gaze locked on the sensual curves of his lips. "I, uh, forgot my guidebook inside."

"You don't need one. I can tell you everything you want to know."

The empty promise pulled at her like a black hole. "Everything?"

One corner of his mouth quirked up. "Let's just enjoy this sunny afternoon, okay?"

How could he turn her brain to jelly with just half a smile? "All right." For now. They all needed this calm before the storm.

Rosane bounced along ahead on the sidewalk with Armand. Her fuchsia coat offered the only color in their ill-assorted group. Armand, in his usual style, wore a black fur hat, a black woolen scarf and a black calf-length wool coat over his black suit. When had his choice of clothing mutated in her mind from gentlemanly to sinister? All this talk of scars and fear and death was to blame. She glanced at Daniel. And him.

He matched his somber mood with charcoal jeans, a dark ski jacket and black hiking boots. Sunglasses hid his eyes—against the sun or the crowd?

Even she didn't add any color. Her cream-colored coat hid a gray sweater and matched the dirty snow banking the sidewalk. The hard heels of her black boots clicked on the slushy cement in time to her worried thoughts. She should have worn red or purple or a vibrant blue that would charge her with energy.

For now, the two men seemed content to let their differences lie. For that, Christi was thankful. She walked beside Daniel with her gloved hands stuffed deep into her coat pockets, making sure their elbows didn't accidentally touch. Was it too early to sneak a Tums? Lunch already swirled in an acid soup around her stomach.

The cold air nipped at her nose, but the sun's strong rays warmed her face. The clear soft blue of the sky reminded her of the baby blanket in which she'd carried Rosane home. Keeping her gaze off Daniel, she played with her breath, delighting in the locomotive-like bursts of steam. Staying distracted was better than letting her mind dwell on remembered kisses or all the questions snaking through her head when it came to Daniel.

But he made ignoring him difficult with the insistent swish of his sleeves rubbing against his jacket. It sang a rhythm, becoming a constant reminder of his proximity—of her illogical desire for closeness. If he had this effect on all his female admirers, it was no wonder the women at the party had flocked to him and drooled over his music.

The man had presence. Had it even at twenty. It wasn't that he was handsome. His nose was too long, his cheekbones too sharp and his chin too square. But the sense of purpose, the aura of success was evident, and if she dared admit it, a bit overwhelming.

Although Daniel had said he wanted to protect her, in the game he played with Armand, pawns were easy to sacrifice. And in Daniel's arms, she could easily forget they both had something important to lose.

Armand and Rosane walked ahead, deep in conversation, pausing now and then to look at something of interest. The houses gave way to a stand of evergreens, then to a wide field spread thick and white like frosting on a cake. Away from the protection of trees and houses, the wind picked up intensity and whipped at her hair. She lifted the hood of her jacket to cover her head.

Daniel wrapped an arm around her shoulder. "Cold?"

She shook her head. His touch was dangerous. Already her pulse quickened and her temperature shot up, making her coat seem redundant. They were in public; she was safe.

With a somber gaze that suggested dark brooding, Daniel glanced over her head at the field as they walked. ''How much do you know of your Canadian history?''

''Not much.''

He squeezed her shoulder gently and stopped walking. Facing the field, he placed her before him. His right arm came over her shoulder and his hand pointed to the white expanse of snow.

''These are known as the Plains of Abraham. They're part of the Battlefield Park.''

As he told his tale of a battle fought long ago, she could see the redcoats struggling up the steep face of rock from the St. Lawrence River. Quiet ants in the heart of the night, edging toward a deadly picnic. How many had sensed their impending deaths? How many had sensed victory? Had they, like her, felt their souls shrink as their minds battled between desire and duty? She envied the soldier's quick deaths on the battlefield. Daniel's every touch killed her much too slowly.

''By morning they'd blocked the supply lines and the French had to come out in the open and fight,'' Daniel continued, unaware her every thought centered on him. ''On this field right here. Wolfe came from that direction and Montcalm from there.''

His right arm pointed toward one end of the field. His left arm came up and swept toward the citadel, which he informed her, the British built later. Her nose was ice-cold. Her back, where their bodies touched, sizzled red-hot. The woodsy scent of his aftershave filled her nostrils and his breath tickled her ear, making it hard for her to concentrate on his words.

"In a bloody fifteen minute battle, Canada's fate was decided. It was now under British rule." His tone changed from serious to teasing. "Some say that if Montcalm hadn't been so eager to spend the night with his mistress, the outcome of the battle would've been quite different."

He held her tightly, transmitting an urgency that belied the light mood and sent a wave of panic surging through her. "As it was, both Wolfe and Montcalm were mortally wounded. In the Parcs des Gouverneurs, near the Château Frontenac, there's a monument honoring both the winner and the loser. It's the only statue of its kind in the world."

She tried to hold on to his earlier teasing tone. "You sound like a tour guide."

"I should. I worked as one for two summers."

She cocked her head to look up at him. "Really? I can't picture you doing that."

"A handsome guy like me?"

His amusement reverberated against her spine like a strand of precious pearls. How could anyone resist that soft laughter? "I'll just bet you got great tips."

"It didn't hurt that I understood English."

She managed to squeeze an inch of space between their bodies as she feigned interest in the battle's location. His arms were still draped over her shoulders, making her aware of every inch of her skin. His touch had the ability to render her both senseless and alive. A contradiction that confused her as much now as it had nine years ago. A sough of wind breathed across the plain and ruffled the ends of her hair. She shivered.

Daniel kissed the top of her hood. "I won't bore you any more with history lessons."

Lessons, she had a feeling, that spoke of more than a battle fought long ago. She pushed herself from his arms. With the toe of one boot, she drew a pattern on the snowbank. "Talk to me, Daniel."

Thrusting his hands into the pockets of his jacket, he looked at her long and deep. For an instant she thought she could see right through the lenses of his sunglasses into his soul. Then a dark cloud of sorrow shrouded his features, taking him a galaxy away from her. "History marks."

Every bit of winter crept into her bones. The acid in her stomach popped and fizzed like some potent witch's brew. She rolled the pack of Tums along her palm. "Say what you mean."

His shoulders hiked up. Every line of his body steeled, poised against a coming blow. He seemed to swallow a hard knot lodged at the base of his throat. "I'm not denying my heritage. I am who I am because of where I was born and who I was born to. If I hadn't been born with my country's history, would my music be the same? Probably not. Just as if I'd been born to different parents, I wouldn't—" He shrugged and shook his head, shutting the creaking door of emotions he'd barely opened.

"You're wrong. People are what they make themselves to be." She'd learned that lesson every time her family pulled up barely grafted roots to transplant themselves in some new and alien soil.

"Speaking from experience?"

"Yes." At the force of her conviction one of his eyebrows shot up. Her gaze wandered to Rosane, who skipped around Armand while he walked with the careful gait of someone whose bones hurt. "History shapes us, but it doesn't define us. We do that for ourselves."

Daniel followed the track of her gaze. "Then why do your roots matter so much to you?"

"Because if you don't know where you come from, you can't make informed choices."

Daniel nodded once. When he took her hand to continue walking, she let him. He'd opened up—just a crack in that wall as thick as the citadel protecting the city. Did she dare prod for more? "What is it about your past that hurts you so much?"

He took in a sharp breath. His answer was a swallowed explosion. "The betrayal."

In that moment, she understood how the razor-sharp wire of his grief had fenced his heart. The betrayal or who had betrayed him didn't matter. She just wanted to snip the tight strands of bloody wire, to sand away the sharp edges that dug so deep. She wanted him to know that he wasn't alone.

"Daniel…" She reached for his cheek with a gloved hand.

He leaned his face into the palm of her hand. "Hmm?"

"Tonight." She cradled the small offered weight of his trust. "I'll tell Rosane who you are."

THE CHEERFUL tour guide was back, Christi thought when they reached an area crowded like a beehive and buzzing with activity. Daniel pointed to a huge snow structure across the street. "How do you like that?"

"It looks like a castle," Rosane said, holding on

to one of Daniel's and one of Armand's hands—a safety between two loaded guns.

"It *is* a castle. Bonhomme Carnaval lives here during the Carnaval."

Constructed of snow blocks, the ice castle stood about three stories high. Red and white flags adorned its towers. Gray metal barriers guarded the structure and directed the flow of pedestrian traffic. The sun glinted off the white surface, making the castle shine like a giant crystal. People milled around, enjoying the hidden passages inside.

"We'll stop on the way back." Daniel smiled down at his daughter, and once again the ghost of the young man she'd fallen for came alive. "You might enjoy shaking hands with Bonhomme."

On their side of the street, rows of ice sculptures were in the final stages of construction. Men and women perched on tall ladders rasped and planed details into hard-packed blocks of snow. Christi marveled at the ingenuity that had gone into the various pieces—everything from a dancing bear, to political figures to shapes defying both description and gravity.

Farther ahead, clowns and mascots entertained children between races, rides and sledding runs. A woman dressed in a snow fairy's costume painted faces. Rosane looked to Christi for permission. At her nod, Daniel handed Rosane a loonie, a dollar coin, to pay for the glittery snowflake design she chose. It covered all of one cheek and sparkled in the sun.

The odd quartet resumed their walk and passed the stone archway into the old part of the city. Daniel rattled off the historic importance of everything from houses to a cannonball buried at the base of a tree.

The shops along rue St. Louis were brightly decorated for the festivities, inviting passersby for a closer look.

Armand and Rosane disappeared into a gift shop. She came out clutching a stuffed plush snowman that wore a red cap and a brightly colored sash around his waist. "Look, Mom, a Bonhomme Carnaval." She looked up at Armand. "Did I say that right?"

"You said it perfectly."

She beamed.

Then Armand caught sight of something across the street and his face became a maze of lines that reflected his age. Daniel followed Armand's gaze and tensed.

"If you'll excuse me for a moment," Armand said, then crossed the street and went inside a restaurant with a bright red door.

Christi's thumb counted the ridges marking each tablet on the roll of antacid in her pocket. "What's wrong?"

"Trouble," Daniel said, swallowing the word as if it were bile.

"What kind of trouble?"

He ignored her. "You and Rosane keep going. I'll catch up." He waited for a bus to trundle by, then jogged across the street to the restaurant Armand had entered.

When the haze of diesel fumes cleared, Christi saw inside the well-lit entrance of the restaurant. Armand was speaking to a short, but muscular man when Daniel confronted him. The man Armand talked to dipped his cap in salutation and made a quick exit.

Once outside, the capped man looked in her direction. She shivered as his eyes blinked, making her feel photographed and memorized. Instinctively, she clasped Rosane close to her. The man zipped his jacket against the cold and sped away in the opposite direction.

Her attention focused back to the restaurant's open door. The explosion she'd dreaded all afternoon detonated before her eyes. Daniel and Armand gestured wildly as the maître d' frantically tried to umpire the pair out the door.

Christi grabbed Rosane's hand and propelled her forward. "What did you and Armand talk about?"

Rosane shrugged as her eyes darted from bright window display to bright window display. "Things."

"What kind of things?"

"About school and my friends." Rosane held up her stuffed snowman and fingered the sash. "He says this fancy sash on Bonhomme is called a *ceinture fléchée*."

There was no reason for Armand to confide in a child, but it was worth a shot. She cranked her gaze over her shoulder in the direction of the restaurant. What were they arguing about? What kind of trouble was the capped man? Was he part of Armand's plan? She couldn't stand the suspense of not knowing anymore, but had to settle for a Tums to ease her tension.

She didn't see any of the store windows at which they lingered and barely heard Rosane's continuous chatter. When Rosane stopped, fascinated by a shop worker dressed as a lumberjack who poured hot maple syrup over a manger of homemade snow, Christi glanced once more in the direction of the restaurant. People pushed and shoved as they made their way on the crowded sidewalk and she could no longer see the restaurant's bright red door. Rosane tugged at

Christi's sleeve and pointed toward the snow toffee. "Can I? Pe-lease?"

Christi handed her some money, then popped another Tums. What was taking them so long?

A calèche clopped by, momentarily distracting her. The shaggy bay's bells jingled, and a couple, snuggled under a fur, kissed as the driver urged the horse into a trot.

Once the carriage passed, Christi finally picked Daniel and Armand out of the crowd. Both had stubborn expressions etched into their faces. Both walked with stiff strides. Daniel's face remained clouded as they approached, but Armand's transformed itself once more into the gracious host.

"I hope we have not kept you waiting too long," he said with exaggerated civility.

"No, we've enjoyed window shopping," she lied.

"If you would like to purchase anything, I can arrange to have your purchases delivered."

"Thank you, but I'm not in a buying mood today."

Rosane, unaware of the tension in her adult companions, busily licked every drop of congealed maple syrup from the squat wooden spoon. "I'm going to keep this stick so I can remember how good snow tastes."

Christi winced when Rosane carefully placed the sticky spoon in the pocket of her coat, but said nothing.

"Who was the man at the restaurant?" Christi asked Armand as if the answer didn't matter one bit.

Rosane stuck her hand in Armand's and reached for one of Daniel's as they started walking again.

"Célestin Cadieu. He is a private investigator I often employed to do background research on prospective parents. I felt responsible for every child I placed in private adoption.''

Daniel shot Armand a black look that would have reduced a less secure adversary to dust. The stir of his anger was alive with an energy that had her pulse knocking through her gut. In spite of her fear of a repeated explosion, Christi pushed on. ''Oh, do you still have an office? I thought you'd retired.''

''I am retired. I gave up my office a few years ago. But there was a problem with one of the last adoptions I handled. I am trying to rectify the situation so the child will not suffer from the unexpected loss of her adoptive parents.''

''Oh.'' Christi could think of nothing else to say. Of all the things she'd expected this was the last. Could a man with such selfless motives toward a baby for which he no longer had any responsibility really want to cause her harm? Had she misunderstood all she'd heard that morning between Daniel and Armand?

I saw Caroline's scar. She frowned. What scar? How did all these tangled lines fit together?

Daniel, choosing peace, it seemed, resumed his monologue on the mosaic of tall, narrow, cut-stone buildings they passed. Seeing Rosane's delight at all the new sights she took in pleased Christi and allowed her a notch of relaxation.

When they reached the Château Frontenac, Rosane announced she had to go to the bathroom, and Armand insisted on taking her inside.

''We'll all go,'' Christi said, loathe to let Rosane out of her sight.

''I will make sure no harm comes to your daughter,'' Armand said as if he sensed her discomfort.

"The old and the young tire much more easily than healthy adults like you. I know you would like to see more of the city, and Daniel would be pleased to show you. Rosane and I will have a hot chocolate in the hotel restaurant, then I shall call a taxi to take us home."

Home. It sounded so good, so warm, so…solid. He did look tired. So did Rosane. He was an old man. He was dying. He wanted to know his family—just as she did. And his request sounded so reasonable. How could she refuse without arousing his suspicion? If he really did mean her harm, then she had to make him think she knew nothing of his plans or she wouldn't get the chance to continue her investigation. And since he no longer kept an office, the evidence— or lack thereof—was somewhere in the house. The basement? The attic? Even if all she did was prove Daniel wrong, then it was worth it for the peace of mind. Either way, she had to know.

Before she could answer, Rosane tugged on Armand's hand. "Let's go!"

"Rosie—"

Rosane stomped one foot and cocked her hands against her hips. "Oh, Moooom, I'm big enough to go to the bathroom by myself."

"I know, honey, I just wanted to remind you to behave for Armand."

"I'm always good." She tugged on Armand's hand again. "I gotta go!"

Christi waved at her daughter, but Rosane didn't look back.

"Are you sure that's wise?" Daniel's voice vibrated close to her ear, an echo of her uncertain conscience.

She turned to face him. "If you're right. If Armand does want to harm me, then he needs my trust. What better way to gain it than to treat my daughter like a princess? Rosane is safe with him."

"Hurt comes in all sorts of packages, Christiane. Armand's an expert at inflicting scars no one can see."

"Then talk to me, Daniel. Give me an example. Show me all the dire consequences of my decision."

Like a stone wall, Daniel's blank face deflected the barrage of her anger. "Be reasonable."

"I think I've been more than reasonable. I gave you what you wanted. And you're paying me back by not trusting me."

"He'll hurt her."

Her hands gestured like caged birds suddenly released. "How do you know? How can you be so sure? According to you, it's me he's obsessed with, not her. What would he gain by hurting her? Before he could do anything, I'd leave. He'd die before he ever found me again. Where would that leave his plans?"

"Christiane—"

"You want me to marry you, but how can I when what you're offering feels…borrowed? That's what I've had my whole life—borrowed friends, borrowed towns, borrowed stories. I want something real for Rosane and me. Something we can keep forever. Something that's ours. Marriage is a partnership. I won't accept it any other way."

His body vibrated with stiff control on the cusp of shattering and his voice was full of edges. "Christiane—"

"It's a deal breaker, Daniel." She shoved her

hands into her coat pocket and wrapped her fingers around what remained of the roll of antacid. "Either we talk or you walk away and don't ever come back."

ARMAND LOWERED himself into the padded dining room chair. Tourists and shoppers crowded the restaurant, but his influence still meant something. They got a seat by the window. He saw Daniel and Christiane arguing outside and smiled. *That's it, Daniel. That's what I had in mind.*

The afternoon started to take its toll and weariness crept into his old bones. He was glad Mardi Gras was near. His deteriorating body became more difficult to live in every day. Growing old was still a surprise to him. He ordered a hot chocolate for Rosane and an Irish coffee for himself.

"How did you like the Château's shops?" he asked Rosane, who busily stuffed her purple hat and mittens into her coat pocket.

"I loved it! Especially the one with that sparkly castle." She hung her coat on the back of the chair.

"Maybe if you are good, I will buy it for you."

"I'm always good."

She *was* always good. He found that quality charming in a child, but in this instance, it was becoming a problem.

He found his handkerchief and screened a coughing fit with it. "I think I am getting a cold."

"Then you should've ordered tea. Mom always gives me tea with honey and lemon when I have a cold."

A chuckle rumbled through his chest. "You have a smart mother."

A uniformed waiter served their order. Rosane's eyes grew wide at the mound of whipped cream towering high on top of the cup.

"How is your hot chocolate?"

Rosane struggled to figure out how to dig into the concoction. "Great! Mom puts marshmallow in hers, but I think I like this whipped cream better." She took a large spoonful and carefully guided the cloud of cream into her mouth. Some of it listed to one side, leaving a tiny white mustache on her upper lip. She licked it clean.

Armand took a long sip from his drink and let the hot coffee warm his throat and the glow of the whiskey seep into his tired bones. He'd arranged for thousands of adoptions, but the closest he'd come to knowing children was his acquaintance with Daniel and his sister, Lise.

A deeper knowledge of children would serve him well right now. He needed to direct this planned conversation carefully. He must broach the delicate subject of her parentage with the right amount of innocence so that she would still trust him, yet with enough punch for her to resent Daniel and harbor a grudge against her mother. She had to take enough offense at his revelation to give Christiane a reason to worry.

He drank from his cup, sipping in inspiration. "Does your mother ever talk of your father?"

"He's dead."

When Rosane started kicking an annoying rhythm on the leg of her chair, he blocked his mind to the noise and concentrated instead on the child's face. "What did she tell you about him?"

"He was very handsome and very kind. He was a

music student, you know.'' She scooped another spoonful of whipped cream and savored it.

''Doesn't that sound like someone you know?''

She cocked her head for a moment as if considering the question, then shook her head. ''Nope.''

''Daniel is a musician, too. Just like your father.'' He paused to let the words sink in. ''Do you like Daniel?''

She shrugged. ''He's teaching me to skate. He plays hockey, you know.''

''Yes, and he's good at it.''

She stopped kicking the chair and excavated her drink from a fresh angle.

''Did you notice how you look a bit like Daniel?''

She laughed as if the notion tickled her. ''You're so silly!'' Another mound of cream bobbed its way into her mouth. She placed the spoon on the linen tablecloth, then picked up the cup with both hands and tested the hot liquid.

What now? He took a fortifying swallow from his drink. ''Perhaps your father is not dead.''

Her cup stopped in midair. She stared right through him. ''My father is dead. My mother told me.''

''Your father is Daniel.''

She brought the cup down on the saucer with a clang. ''My mom doesn't lie to me.''

Her brow furrowed and her fists tightened around the delicate china cup. He was afraid it might break under her grasp.

''She thought it might hurt you to know Daniel left when he found out about you. She did not want you to know your father did not want you when you were a baby.'' He kept his tone soothing, hypnotic. Hadn't it worked with all the young girls fat with child and lean on prospects?

Rosane drew back into the protective shell she'd worn when she'd first arrived. Not good. He needed her to take her anger out on her mother.

Forehead crimped like an old turtle, she sipped tentatively. Her gaze stayed fixed on a lonely iceberg tip of cream floating on the surface of the cocoa ocean.

"I think it is better that you know." Armand emptied his cup and toyed with the idea of ordering a glass of wine. "You are a big girl. You should know everything that concerns you." He reached across the table to touch the soft skin of her hand. "Your mother wants you to like Daniel so they can marry."

Her gaze jerked up, raw fear zigzagging like lightning in her gray eyes. She slammed her cup against the saucer, chipping off a piece of the stem.

"Wouldn't you like to live with Daniel here? Like a family?"

The cup she still held rattled in its saucer. She kicked at the chair in double time. There was something stoic, yet helpless and boxed-in about the way tears gleamed in her eyes, but didn't fall. Oh, she was strong, so strong. It was a pity he didn't have the time to wait for her to mature. She gave the chocolate one last swirl, then pushed the cup away. "Can we go now?"

"Don't you want to know your father?"

She tugged mitts and cap from her coat pocket and placed them on the table's edge. "I like things just the way they are."

"Then you need to tell your mother. Your feelings are important to her. She will be glad to know how sad her plans make you feel."

She was such a lovely child. Seeing her hurt caused a twinge of guilt. ''Would you like another hot chocolate?''

''No, thank you. Can we go home now?''

''Would you like to stop and get that crystal palace first?''

''Sure.'' Rosane shrugged as she retrieved her coat from the back of the chair. She put it on, crammed her hat on her head, drew her mittens over her hands, and scooped up the stuffed Bonhomme next to the chair almost as an afterthought.

He sighed as he buttoned his coat. Her pain was a temporary necessity. The discomfort would soon fade. In the meantime, it would keep Christiane too busy to wonder about his plans. And after he gained eternal life, he would make sure Rosane was never again sad.

Chapter Seven

Daniel fielded Christiane's words like barroom blows. He could take abuse as well as the next person. Lord knows he'd spent enough time on the receiving end of bruising speech and scraping fists. But here, on a sidewalk crawling with tourists, was not the place. And coming from her, it set off a firework of feelings he didn't know how to orchestrate.

When Christiane collided against him to charge to the hotel where Armand sat with Rosane, the hood of her coat fell back, exposing her moonlight-blond hair. His hands reached out, capturing her arms. Sound rumbled in his chest, then rasped in his throat and came out a stranger. "Christiane, wait."

The vulnerable hurt in the quicksilver pools of her eyes tugged at his conscience.

"Why is it so hard for you to speak your heart?" Her voice cracked like thin ice over a raging river.

"Words hurt."

"Unsaid, they hurt more because imagination gives them weight."

The cold breeze whispered through her short locks, rippling the strands in time to her quickened breaths. His heart boomed against his chest and the angry thunder ripping through him twined with the strange longing that seemed to always consume him when she was near. Even the thick callus of skin he'd grown couldn't stop him from bleeding on the inside.

What did she want? To hear that he'd looked for her in every crowd he'd performed for? That his love for her kept him boxed in a maze with no exit? That seeing her in Armand's house turned him inside out and left him raw with dread?

She wanted words, but they wouldn't give her what she needed. He could already taste her disappointment, sharp and brassy, on his tongue, and just as strongly, he yearned for her remembered sweetness. Why did she need words when the pull between them was stronger than gravity? Why did she need words that would let her down when the truth was there in every touch? Why did she need words when he could give her all she needed?

He captured her lips in a kiss and hoped she heard her answers shared heartbeat-to-heartbeat. A moan of anguish rolled low in her throat, even as her arms freed themselves from his hold and her fingers tangled themselves in his hair.

A familiar symphony of sensations arose—cellos of longing, saxophones of sensuality, trumpets of warning. His physical awareness of the music of her pulse was so intense, he prayed it would fill that empty chasm time had spanned between them.

He'd tried to forget her. He'd tried to lose himself in his music. He'd tried running from city to city, using tours as excuses. But always she was on his mind. Holding her in his arms was like coming home after a long fight. Except that the fighting wasn't done and she'd soon pull out the welcome mat.

Instead of freeing them, the conversation they were not having was widening the crevice between them.

She pulled away from him, sadness a turbulent pool in her eyes. On her tongue, his name was a quiet puff of desperation. "Daniel." She shook her head. "This is not a good idea."

The only way to build a bridge over the precipice, the only way to keep her safe was to give a truth that would hurt her. Some mistakes nothing could hide, not even the best of intentions.

"Let's go to my mother's gallery," he said, frowning at the gawking stares of recognition and agitated whispers of passersby pressing in for a closer look. Would the gossip rags postulate about the mysterious blonde Daniel Moreau was seen kissing in the middle of Old Quebec? "It's nearby. I'm sure she'll let us use her office." The walk would give him a chance to think.

Nodding, Christiane reached into her coat pocket and extricated a roll of Tums. She ripped at the wrapper and popped two tablets into her mouth.

"Have you seen anyone about your stomach problem?" he asked as he led her across the street.

She shrugged. "I'm fine."

"That's hard to believe with the amount of antacid I've seen you go through today."

She jammed her hands into her pockets and kicked at an errant pebble. "My stomach makes too much acid. It's sometimes bothersome, but not dangerous."

Stress, he thought. And he was going to add to it.

Silently they wound their way down the rue du Fort and the Côte de la Montagne. When they reached the Escaliers Casse-Cou, Daniel took Christiane's arm so she wouldn't slip on the snowy stairs. They weren't called breakneck for nothing.

Le Petit Cartier Champlain was a quaint shopping area that had brought some of the oldest houses in Canada back to life. His mother's art gallery was sandwiched between a chocolate shop and one that sold decorative copper.

"My mother has a talent for discovering new artists. She keeps all kinds of art from soapstone sculptures to woven tapestries." He chuckled as he opened the bright yellow door and was greeted by the tinkling of sleigh bells. "At first it'll look like chaos, but you'll soon see a kind of mad order to everything."

As they entered, the birch wood slats of the gallery floor creaked. The scent of spiced apples surrounded them in welcome. He spotted his mother in an animated discussion with a client who looked torn between two paintings. Her need for art was as great as his for music, and he loved seeing her in action. As she pointed out the virtues of the two modern art paintings to her customer, her brown eyes were ablaze with excitement. One would have thought she were the artist. Her shoulder-length chestnut hair, salted with a few strands of gray, was caught by a bright silk scarf in a ponytail that bobbed back and forth as she turned her head from customer to painting, treating them both with equal respect.

Chantal Moreau had bloomed after her husband's death. The haggard defeated look she'd worn during his childhood had disappeared overnight, as if the ground swallowing her captor's coffin had set her free. When Daniel's music had finally given him the opportunity to offer her a new career, she'd jumped at the chance to own her own gallery and promote the interest in art that had sustained her through her difficult marriage. A marriage she'd endured for the sake of her children.

She didn't know at what price her happiness had come. And he'd never tell her.

CHRISTI SCANNED the wall of Le Petit Coin while Daniel went to his mother. He was right; the gallery was a mishmash of unmatched art.

She spotted a shelf of native Canadian sculptures interspersed with clay figurines and modern pieces that looked as if someone had fashioned them from scrap. There was a wall of paintings ranging from precise watercolor landscapes to blobs of colors splattered haphazardly on canvases. Textured tapestries hung on another wall. The floor was crowded with racks of leather crafts, quilts, hand-woven shawls and batik scarves. Daniel's mother had wide ranging tastes. With one hand, Christi shredded the remains of the pack of antacid and let the bits of paper and foil fall to the bottom of her pocket.

Another creak from the floor brought attention to their presence. Daniel's mother beamed when she saw her son. Her petite figure was clad in dress slacks that swished with every move and a thigh-length wildly colored tunic that matched the scarf holding her ponytail. Christi smiled at the eccentric earrings at her lobes. They had a taste for odd jewelry in common.

"Daniel, did you get your phone fixed?" Her French was soft, lilting, teasing.

"It's not broken." He kissed her on both cheeks.

"Oh, I thought it must be. You haven't called since you got back." She peeled the sunglasses off his face and handed them to him.

"I haven't had a chance."

She slanted Christi a curious look and a knowing smile.

Daniel hooked the stem of his sunglasses onto the neck of his sweater. "I've been at Armand's."

She sucked in her cheeks and her grasp around Daniel's arms became manacle tight. "Why on earth would you do such a thing?"

"It's a long story." He introduced his mother to her. Christi plucked a smile from some deep reserve, and they shook hands with cautionary care.

Christi hadn't missed the quick appraisal the older woman gave her. Why should she care if Daniel's mother liked her? It wasn't as if they were truly bound by her son. Her lungs suddenly felt too tight. They *were* bound—through Rosane. This woman was her daughter's grandmother.

"Can we use your office for a few minutes?" Daniel asked.

"Of course." Her answer was filled with questions. She glanced at her client, then back at Daniel, clearly torn between the two.

Daniel gave her a little push in her client's direction. "Go. We'll catch up later."

The office was snug, but tastefully decorated. A swag of ivy-printed material hung over an otherwise bare window. Neat piles of paper were strewn over an antique rosewood desk and a computer blinked on a rolling cart beside it. Behind the desk, a stack of shelves filled with books on art, accounting and business covered the wall. Two walnut file cabinets flanked the shelves. Ivy hung from a ceramic pot in the corner, while a coffeepot on top of one of the cabinets filled the room with warmth.

Daniel poured two mugs of coffee, handed one to her and sat on the corner of the desk, offering her a chair. She wrapped her hands around the mug and let the warm ceramic thaw her frozen fingers.

"Ask what you want and I'll try to answer." His words didn't match his stance; he looked ready to bolt.

In the timid light of the room, the brandy of his eyes had almost disappeared, leaving wide black pupils. She pushed the mug of coffee onto the desk and leaned forward for a closer look. But the mirror she'd expected was nothing but a dark curtain. After all these years, they'd each grown layers of self-protection. Peeling them back would take time.

"The truth?" she asked, uncertain he could bring himself to talk openly.

"As much as I can."

Her heart beat a fast cadence in her chest, reminding her inanely of one of Daniel's wilder compositions. She pinched the lining of her pockets afraid to raise her hopes only to have them lopped off at the root. "Why did you leave?"

Her heart still bled at the remembered pain. How many days had she run to the mailbox expecting to find a letter from him? How many evenings had she waited by the phone hoping to hear his voice? How many nights had she lain awake crying for him?

"You knew I was only there for a short stay."

"I deserved a goodbye."

"I couldn't." His brows, furrowed in pain, matched the knots gnarled in her gut.

"Why?"

He moved behind the desk as if he couldn't trust himself near her. "Do you remember the night I picked you up at the ice-cream parlor? You'd spilled a milk shake over your sweater and you wanted to change.''

"How could I forget?" Her fingers crimped more tightly around the lining of her pockets. "I went upstairs to change and by the time I came back down, you were gone."

"Armand had offered me a scholarship. Music was the only piece of sanity in my life. Texas Christian University. The home of the Van Cliburn competition. Can you see how the pull was irresistible?"

He'd always had big dreams and an even bigger drive. A part of her had known that, however much she meant to him, she would always come second to his music.

"There's a price for everything," he said, his voice rough with regret. "I thought what he asked for in return was nothing. I remember laughing at my good fortune. A full ride. And all I had to do was become your friend."

In spite of the warmth, she shuddered. "I don't understand."

He shoved the mug of coffee onto the file cabinet and braced his palms against the edge of the desk. His words came out tentatively as if he were tiptoeing through a minefield. "Armand. He'd told me you were his illegitimate daughter."

"What?" She had her father's blond hair, not Armand's dark features. She had her father's temper, his mannerisms, his stubbornness. Armand couldn't *be* her father, could he?

"He said he wanted a chance to meet you and talk to you. He said your mother wouldn't allow him contact because she was ashamed of what had happened between them."

"That's crazy!" Was that why Caroline ran? Was that why she was constantly looking over her shoulder? Was that why she wouldn't speak of her childhood?

"He held our financial well-being, don't you see? My mother's, my sister's and mine." Daniel tight-walked through the words she'd forced out of him. "When my father died eleven years ago, all he left us was debt. My mother worked two jobs to try and pay it all back. My sister had to give up medical school. They'd both suffered enough. I could set them free. I could have my dream and theirs, too."

He lifted his hands in a helpless gesture. "All I had to do was bring you back to Quebec City for a visit. It seemed so little for all I was getting in return."

A dire foreboding rose from a dark corner in the cavern of her heart, then bottomed before the ache there could knock her flat. She searched his face for the truth. "Was nothing between us real?"

"It was much too real." He stared out the window. He tried to lose himself in the dark of dusk smothering the alley behind his mother's shop, but he couldn't escape Christiane's haunted reflection on the glass. With every word that fell out of his mouth, the lines of her became more faint. By the time he was done would she be nothing more than a ghost? He rubbed at the ache at his breastbone. "That night. Your parents were both home."

The recognition of the oddity registered on her face. Her father always worked late. "Your father had a background search done on me. That's why he was home early."

"He what?" Her hands jumped out of the pockets of her coat and grasped the arms of the chair. Her body seemed poised to follow, then dropped back in the seat as if it were too heavy for her to lift.

"When your mother heard her past in my accent, she became concerned. To ease her mind, your father offered the search. When she saw that my father was Armand's partner, that they'd worked together, she grew worried. She asked me why I was here, why I'd chosen you. While you were upstairs, she told me Armand had tried to kill her. She showed me the scar on her chest."

Denial had Christiane shaking her head. "She had no scar. I never saw a scar."

He cut an invisible slash from the top of his breastbone to his sternum, tracing the length of scar he couldn't erase from his memory. "Did you ever see her wear anything low-cut? A bathing suit? A dress with a plunging neckline?"

The truth sprang to her eyes as she flipped through the pages of her memory and remembered the sleeveless turtlenecks, the Chinese collars, the dresses with the gathered fronts that tied high around the neck. Christiane had shown him the albums of her life. He crouched beside her chair and, in his mind, turned the pages with her.

"There're a million good reasons for her choice of wardrobe." Her voice was a rickety whisper. "Why did you believe her story about how she got the scar?"

"In her eyes I saw the depth of her fear." He rubbed Christiane's arms compulsively, as if that could warm the chill shivering her limbs. "She begged me. She told me that if I loved you, I should leave. If Armand ever found you, he would kill you.''

Her hands knotted and unknotted on her lap like lost spiders. ''You could have stayed. You could have told Armand you never met me. You could—''

''I knew what he was capable of. I'd seen his work. He tore my family apart with his greed. He used my father's weakness for young girls to feed his business. After my father died, he used me to feed his obsession.'' Daniel took her restless hands in his, pressed them against his heart. ''I loved you, Christiane. My mind, my heart, my music was full of you. I couldn't let him harm you. I bought your freedom. Can't you understand that?''

''No, I don't. You bought it with what?''

He'd always known what price he'd pay when he chose to leave. It wasn't a decision he'd made lightly. But it was the last one he'd made with his heart. ''With my scholarship.''

Her eyes widened. Her mouth opened in a narrow *O*. ''Daniel, no.''

His throat worked around the knot lodged there. He didn't want her pity. Dreams were mutable. ''I didn't need Armand's money anyway. My only regret was that my mother had to keep her factory job, and my sister's schooling took twice as long as it should because she had to work.''

''And you?''

He tried to return her hands to her, but she curled her fingers around the wool of his sweater, cradling the bruised beats of his heart. ''I did what I could.'' Anger had driven him as much as ambition. And the anger he expressed with his fists had gotten him into a lot of trouble. Of course, it had also brought Jean-

Paul his way, and Jean-Paul had found a way to channel both the anger and the raw talent into a career. "I worked my way from piano bars to star." If you could call guilt stardom.

"Why couldn't you tell me then?"

Her voice was wet with tears and each one weighed on his heart. He closed his eyes and laid his head in her lap, ashamed of his younger self's cowardice. "Because if I saw you again, I'd never have had the courage to leave. And if I ever tried to see you again, Armand had promised you would suffer as Caroline had."

"Oh, Daniel, what a mess we've made of everything." Her palm nestled against the crown of his head, and he wished for this moment of peace to last an eternity. Then in the space between her heartbeats, he heard the notes of her confusion. "Why did Armand want to kill my mother?"

"She didn't tell me." He sank down on his haunches and stared up at her. "But I'd heard my father say Armand tried to harm Caroline and that's why she ran away."

"How does all this tie to the legend of Rose Latulippe?"

He shook his head. "I don't know yet. Armand's been obsessed with that legend since he was a teenager. Then fixed his obsession on Caroline."

Her hands grabbed his wrists. "But you don't kill someone you're obsessed with. It doesn't make sense. If he thought she was Rose reincarnated, wouldn't he want her alive?"

"I don't know what the death means to Armand, only that it's what he wants from you—just as he tried to get it from your mother." Rising, he lifted her from the chair and held her tightly. "Pack your bags, grab your daughter and leave. It's the only way I can keep you safe."

She leaned her head against his shoulder as if it were a moon pulled in by his gravity. "Armand haunted my mother all of her life. She never stopped looking over her shoulder. I never understood why she was so afraid, but her fear infected me. I hated every move. I hated every new place. I hated having to rip away from every bit of familiarity and start all over again. I need to understand why."

He took her head between his hands. "Then marry me. Get out of that house. Stay with me." He bent his head to kiss her, to drink her in, hoping it would somehow quench the creep of dread gnawing at his bones. "I'll keep you safe."

Ending the connection of their kiss, she shook her head. "No, he can't know that I suspect him of evil intentions. If we have any chance of finding out what Rose means to him, why he wants to harm me, to stop this curse, then we have to be there, in his house." She was forewarned; she would stay vigilant.

"It's too dangerous."

"He's an old man. He's sick."

"Or not. It wouldn't be the first time he's lied. And even if he is, it doesn't make him any less driven. He's ready to kill, to die for what he wants. He doesn't care who he hurts."

She tilted her head, and her gaze, clear and quiet, tracked across his face as if it were a map she was trying to remember. "Okay, I'll marry you."

His heart lifted, then sank, a crash of cymbals. She was giving him what he'd asked for, but somehow, it wasn't what he'd expected. His heart wasn't singing.

It was cold and hard and much too deflated. He'd thought the physical bond would be enough. He'd thought having her in his home would be enough. But from the depths of his mind rose the picture of that house in the woods, of laughter, of music. Just like most of his dreams, it dissolved in a puff of smoke and was gone.

To keep her safe, he'd take whatever she gave him.

"Soon," he said. The walls were folding in around him. "Tomorrow."

"No. I need to tell Rosane first. And if Armand thinks I'm busy planning a wedding, he won't be on guard. It'll buy us time."

Then why did it feel as if the hourglass was already empty?

WHEN CHRISTI wound her arms around her daughter that night in the cold cocoon of her room, Rosane pulled away, rounding like a turtle into a shell, and pretended to sleep. She'd been like this since Christi had returned to Armand's house. She put it down to a tiring day. Falling back into herself was Rosane's way of coping with too much stimulus. She'd acted this way after a day at the State Fair, a visit to the Fat Stock Show rodeo and her first day of kindergarten. "Don't you want a story?"

"I'm tired." Rosane pulled the sheet, blanket and comforter tight around her shoulders. The scent of roses wafted in a cloud around them.

"Rosie…" Christi smoothed Rosane's freshly washed hair as soft as down beneath her fingers. "There's something I need to talk to you about."

Rosane yawned and reached for the stuffed snowman Armand had bought her.

Christi snuggled closer, curling her body around her daughter's, a wall of covers between them. "Do you remember when you asked me about your father?"

"He's dead."

Christi's hand snapped back as if Rosane had bitten her. "I," she started, wondering where this harsh bomb had come from, then cleared her throat. "I didn't know where he was."

Rosane's stiff silence gave no encouragement.

"When he left, he didn't tell me where he was going. I didn't know what to tell you when you asked, so I made up a story. A fairy tale. Like the ones you liked me to read to you at night. You were just a little girl."

The walls around her seemed to breathe, to listen to every word expectantly as if they, too, had a stake in the outcome. Christi shook away the unease that ruffled down her spine and inched closer to her daughter's warmth.

"Rosie?" Her heart raced and anxiety sloshed around her stomach. She waited for a response, any kind of sign that would tell her what was going on behind her daughter's closed eyes. How would she take the news? Would she ever forgive the embroidery of a fairy tale stitched to appease a worried little girl? "Rosie... Daniel is your father."

"No! My father is *dead!*"

Rosane shriveled away from her, coiling more tightly into herself. Christi sucked in a gasp at the breach that reminded her much too much of the Cesarean that detached her baby from her womb. "I met Daniel when I was very young. We fell in love. Then he had to go."

"I don't care."

"Rosie—"

Rosane flopped over to face her. Outrage screamed through every inch of her stiff frame. "Why didn't he want me?"

Sobs strafed Rosane's chest and scored at Christi's heart. "Oh, no, Rosie. That's not it at all. Oh, baby, he didn't even know you were on your way." She tugged her daughter into her arms. "That's why he wants to marry us. So we can be a family."

Rosane shoved at Christi's chest with both hands. Christi caught the rounding fists. "Honey—"

"No! You lied to me! I don't want you to marry him! I don't want to be his family! I hate you!"

Fighting the barrier of blankets, Rosane's flaying fists, her own dirge of black thoughts, Christi folded herself around her daughter and hung on through the storm. She crooned while her daughter's tears rained down her chest. She whispered words of love in response to each volley of curses. She absorbed every sob into her bones until all that was left was the spent shell of the child who was an extension of herself.

It wasn't until she crept out the door much later, exhausted and empty, that she realized how easy it was to fail the ones you loved most. In that moment, she forgave her mother. She forgave Daniel, too, because she knew her next action would stab him right through the heart.

Chapter Eight

Two days later, Armand intercepted an expected early delivery and toted the box to his office. Anticipation stirred as turbid as lust as he locked the door behind him. Soon. Very soon. He placed the box on his desk, then rubbed his hands together. From the folds of fancy tissue paper he liberated the treasure and shook it free.

"How do you like it, Caro?" Armand held up the ruby-red dress for her approval. He'd thrown open the curtains and the morning's misty light kissed the sequins on the bodice, giving the impression of liquid fire. "I think she will look wonderful in it." He twirled the dress so Caroline's picture could have a good view of all sides of the gossamer skirt.

"The color is not the best for her, but the cut is flattering. And it matches the locket. The Master will be pleased."

Armand carefully set the dress on his desk and gently folded it, making sure each fold was softened by the tissue paper to prevent ugly creases.

"I had a long talk with the Master last night. Rosane would be better, of course. Thirteen is a much more powerful number than twelve. But the Master wants a bride, not a child, and the doctor told me yesterday that the cancer grows faster than he expected.''

Armand gently lifted the folded dress and placed it back in the dressmaker's box. A fit of coughing rattled through him, and he dropped onto the desk chair to recover.

''That stupid doctor could not understand why it did not matter, why I did not want the chemotherapy.'' He chuckled. ''He does not know that in less than a week, I will have what you cheated me out of all those years ago.''

He reached for the photograph and picked it up. ''You cost me my youth, *chère* Caro. I could have been young forever if you had not been so selfish. As it is, I will have to spend eternity in an old man's body. But then, there is the respect an old man garners. Five days, Caro. Think of it. Five days before I reach every man's goal—eternal life on earth.''

Giddy with euphoria, he hurried to the armoire. He removed the shoes from the rack and lifted the false bottom. ''Would you like to see how I am going to do it?'' He took out an artist's pad and turned to the first page. ''It took me a while to get it right, but I think I have finally done it. Ingenious, if I must say so myself.''

He showed Caroline a drawing of a golden cage suspended high above the theater stage. He traced the outline of the cage with his index finger. ''She will not be able to escape as you did.''

He turned the page to a hastily drawn plan of a building. ''I borrowed the theater plans and everything is set. Célestin is getting the cage built to my specifications. It will be ready tomorrow.''

He turned to the next page. "This is how I see the moment of truth. At midnight, the Master will appear, take his bride away and grant me my wish. No one will be able to stop me. I will have it all, Caro. Money. Power. Respect. Did I tell you I learned a new spell? I will have a captive audience. They will not be able to move and Daniel will not be able to stop playing." Armand's laughter evolved into a racking cough that doubled him over the artist's pad. Droplets of blood sprayed over the sheet and glistened like brilliant-cut rubies.

"Of course, there are still a few details to iron out." He wiped the droplets with a handkerchief, throwing the drawn scene in a red haze. "That daughter of yours has a strong will. But I have a surprise for her."

He closed the pad with a snap. "Did you know she's fallen for Daniel again? Oh, don't frown so, *ma chère*. If love were really that powerful, none of these plans would matter. But it isn't. My love for you failed me. And Christiane's love for Daniel will fail her. She will count on him to save her. But he will be as helpless as I was."

Armand replaced the pad in its hiding place and put the false bottom and the row of shoes back in their proper positions. As he unkinked his spine to stand, the sound of car doors slamming charged the air. His lips twitched up. "Ah, right on time."

He strode to the desk and traced a finger along Caroline's jaw. "Don't be so sad, Caro. Soon you will see your daughter again."

CHRISTI WOKE UP from a nightmare as the sun's weak light clawed its way through the half-opened curtains.

From the mist of her dark dream came the lingering picture of her trapped in the devil's arms as he twirled her in a maddened dance to a demented tune. The last piercing notes of the crazed violin and the pops of fireballs bursting at her feet still echoed in the room even though she was wide-awake now.

Armand's obsession was getting to her. She had to figure out how to stop his mad obsession with her before she lost her mind, and she wasn't going to get anywhere snuggled under this nest of covers. She threw her legs over the side of the bed. *A good general knows his playing field,* her father's voice reminded her. That's exactly what she had to do—keep looking at what lay hidden on this bizarre game board. Armand had to have his genealogy records somewhere. He wouldn't have spent a lifetime collecting something to throw it out just because he'd retired.

As obsessed as Armand was with Rose Latulippe, the records had to be close by. She'd already eliminated his office. In the past two days, she'd explored most of the other rooms in the old stone house. That left the attic and the basement. She shivered. Just what she wanted—to play with rats and spiders.

Christi encased the ice that was her skin in layers—silk long underwear, white long-sleeved T-shirt, burgundy V-neck sweater and wool blazer, black corduroy pants and thick socks. Even then, the wind moaning around the corners of the house seemed to reach straight to her bones.

Dealing with Rosane these past few days had been like living in a war zone. She never knew when the next barrage of bombs would fall or how long the next wall of silence would last.

In that way, Rosane was definitely her father's daughter. Daniel was offering the same impenetrable wordless bunker since she'd told him Rosane's reaction to their engagement.

In the crushing weight of their muteness, Christi had turned into the remote island she'd always feared becoming—alone, unwanted, isolated. Maybe it was time to cut her losses and go home.

She sat at the vanity and reached for the silver-handled brush that had once belonged to her grandmother. Was it her imagination or could she really feel the warmth of her grandmother's hand in the aged silver? Sighing, she ran the soft bristles through her sleep-mussed hair.

"I can't," she told her reflection. The unanswered questions would haunt her. And without answers, her life would end up as restless as her mother's.

The door to her room exploded inward, doorknob crashing into the wall, causing a small dent. Rosane shuffled in backward, stringing Fumée along with a length of wool. Was Christi in store for more silent treatment or a fresh peppering of verbal shrapnel? "Hi, honey. You're up early."

"I had breakfast with Armand." Rosane wore her favorite purple sweatshirt over a white turtleneck and jeans. She yipped when the kitten overshot her mark and bit into her stockinged foot instead of the piece of wool. "She's got sharp teeth."

Christi swallowed her relief that the battle between them was finally back in neutral territory. "She didn't mean to hurt you."

"I know." Rosane threw Christi loaded daggers, grabbed the kitten and bounced onto the bed. "Armand said he'd take me to the mascot parade today. Is that okay? He said to ask.''

''What's the mascot parade?'' Christi brushed her hair and studied the shifting landscape of her daughter's face in the mirror.

''It's for kids. It's at twelve-thirty. Isabelle and her mother are coming, too.''

''Who's Isabelle?''

Rosane rolled her eyes. ''Mom, you know! She's the girl that lives next door. She's nine and she's really nice. She's teaching me how to speak French. Want to hear?''

Christi wasn't about to say no to a show of openness. ''Sure.''

''*Bonjour. Bonsoir.* That means good-day and good-night. *Minou.*'' She lifted the kitten, then spun her on her back and stroked her belly. The cat rolled her head back against Rosane's skinny knees, closed her eyes and purred. ''That's what Fumée is. A kitty.''

Just when Christi thought they'd turned the corner and could return to their previous state of acceptance, or at least peaceful tolerance, the dour child reappeared. Rosane pursed her lips and cocked her head impatiently. ''So can I go to the parade or not?''

Christi sighed, placed the brush back on the vanity and turned to face her daughter. The shell was firmly in place and she had no idea how to get through. Even going home wouldn't resolve the situation with Rosane. Daniel would still stand between them whether they were here or not. They could never go back to the fairy tale that had wrapped them in comfort for all these years. Rosane was better off coming to terms with who Daniel was here where she could see him than three thousand miles away where her imagination could transmute suspicions into deep beliefs that could scar.

"You can go. Bring Isabelle and her mother over first so I can meet them, okay?" With company Armand wouldn't do anything to harm Rosane. Image, she'd learned, was important to him. And with Armand and Rosane out this afternoon, she would have the perfect opportunity to explore the cellar.

A long-suffering sigh shuddered out of her daughter's tiny frame. "Okay."

Rosane scooped up her sleeping kitten, skipped to the door and paused there as if she'd just remembered something. "Why are all those people standing outside?"

"What people?"

"The ones out front by the gate."

Like the precursor to lightning, needles of foreboding pricked Christi's skin. She swiveled in the chair, rose with the slow motion of heavy-limbed dread and approached the window as if she were some sort of dime store novel detective. With a finger, she lifted the side edge of the pink curtain and craned her neck to look down the long slope of roof that exposure to the elements had coated with a mottled green patina. On the street a television van stood with its engine rumbling, belching smoke. The satellite dish on the van roof pointed toward the house and seemed to sniff the air for news. On the snow-packed sidewalk stood a small troupe of people leaning expectantly toward the front door. Only the locked black wrought-iron gate with its deadly spikes kept them caged on the outside.

"Who are they?" Rosane asked again.

"I don't know." But their presence here couldn't be good.

"How COULD YOU?" Daniel's voice detonated across the kitchen. Marguerite made her disapproval known with an equally explosive slapping of pan against the stove's surface. *Control, Daniel, control. Don't let Armand get to you. It's all part of his game.*

"What makes you think I had anything to do with the media's presence here?" Armand shook the newspaper he held, then folded it and threw it across the table. The weekly landed beside an untouched plate piled high with waffles drizzled with raspberry sauce. There in black-and-white, above the fold, was a picture of him kissing Christiane in the middle of the sidewalk two days ago. The headline screamed, *Qui est la Blonde Mystère dans les Bras de Daniel Moreau?* Who is the mystery blonde in Daniel Moreau's arms? "It's you who has attracted them with your inappropriate behavior."

As if on cue, the phone in Daniel's pocket bleated. He peeked down and saw his manager's number flash across the window. Just what he didn't need. He didn't care if he never performed another concert. He didn't care if he never cut another record. He didn't care if he lost the fickle public's esteem. But Jean-Paul wouldn't understand, and Armand couldn't if Daniel was to keep Christiane safe and have a chance to earn his daughter's respect.

"We're engaged." Daniel leaned back in his chair in a show of ease he didn't feel. With Rosane's understandably rebellious reaction to his and Christiane's engagement, Christiane had wanted to back out of her promise. For both their sakes, he hadn't let her. He hated having to play by someone else's tune. It made him feel one note behind. "There's nothing sensational about that."

Marguerite freshened his and Armand's coffees. Armand picked up his cup and sipped. The light in his eyes gleamed as if stoked by some inner furnace. "Until they find out about the child."

Daniel's heart stalled, crashed like a dropped gong, then rolled like a bass drum struck by a crazed drummer. "Something else that will mysteriously leak out to the press?"

Armand shrugged. "It doesn't have to."

"What do you want?" Familiar darkness pressed at his chest.

"Concentrate on your music, Daniel. You've neglected your duties. Your piece *must* be ready on time."

"I earned my music on my own. You don't dictate it."

"Think of your daughter. Your career. You have too much at stake to fail."

Christiane was right. To have any chance at beating Armand, he had to let the old man think he was winning the game. "I've never missed a performance."

Armand rose from his chair. "You've tried to best me, Daniel." He shot the stiff sleeves of his black suit jacket. "But remember that you have yet to succeed."

THE ATMOSPHERE in the house had turned to that of brittle ice. Every breath seemed labored. Every move suspect. Every thought a distorted telegraph that had them all acting with exaggerated courteousness. Both Daniel and Armand told her to ignore the knot of people camped out by the front door. Neither offered an explanation for the reporters' presence. If she needed to go out, they would show her the back way to avoid the prying eyes of the media's cameras.

After Armand and Rosane left, the air warmed only marginally. Daniel disappeared into one of the small parlors strung like wooden beads along the first floor of the house to make phone calls. That left Christi alone.

Armed with a flashlight hidden in the pocket of her blazer, she started down the stairs to the basement. It was even colder here than the rest of the house. She paused and carefully closed the door behind her before she reached for the switch on the wall. The light from the three bare incandescent bulbs screwed into beams didn't glow enough to illuminate the top of the stairs or the far reaches of the room.

The ceiling was no more than six feet—enough for her to stand erect, but Daniel and Armand would both have to bend their tall frames to walk without bumping their foreheads on the overhanging support beams. The packed dirt floor swallowed the sound of her steps. Orienting herself, she noticed rows and rows of metal shelving stacked with unlabeled boxes of all shapes and sizes. At first she saw no order in the chaos of neglected metal and cardboard. Then the shelves seemed to straighten and offer corridors arranged in a labyrinth to maximize the use of space.

Filaments of dusty spider silk webbed the corners of shelves and draped beams and some of the boxes in hanks like Spanish moss. The cold damp scent of dirt and that of the black mold growing like scars along the wall itched her nose.

The cellar had the smell of a place ripe with secrets; the look of greed hoarded for greed's sake rather than the stockpiling of treasured memories.

Straight across from the stairs, a well-beaten path on the dirt floor led to a rounded door with tiny square window, a heavy black metal handle and the kind of lock she imagined would require an old-fashioned key with a scrolled head. She tested the handle. Locked. Rising to her tiptoes, she flashed the beam of her light inside. A small table and one lone wooden chair stood in the middle. Three walls of wine racks filled with bottles rimmed the room. A wine cellar.

She turned her light toward the far end of the basement. Ghostly shadows teased. Beady red eyes stared back at her. She choked back a scream when the frightened mouse squeaked, jumped down from its perch and scurried past her to hide beneath the stairs.

To the left of the stairs a series of posts, still and solemn as black guards, seemed to stand watch over the black cavern behind them. She tore at sticky spider webs, pressed her lips tight at the hissing noise her destruction wrought. Lodged under the cover of the steps were half a dozen metal file cabinets coated with dust.

Excitement rippled through her as she tasted success. Armand's affinity for order would cause his downfall. Here in those organized cabinets, she would find her answers.

She pulled on the topmost handle of the first cabinet. Locked. She tried all of them. All locked. She wiped her hands on the thigh of her pants. Flashing her light at the lock with one hand, she popped a Tums into her mouth with the other and wished she'd learned the art of picking locks somewhere along the way. The lock looked simple enough. How hard could it be? She'd seen it done a thousand times on television.

Her hair was too short for bobby pins or a barrette, but she wore thin silver dangling earrings. She took an earring off and inserted the flat end like a key into the first lock. Mouth pursed in concentration, she felt her way around the tumblers.

"What are you doing?"

Christi gasped and whirled to face Daniel. One hand clutched at her heart for fear it would jump right out of her chest.

"Don't you *ever* do that again!"

"I didn't mean to scare you. What are you doing?" Daniel rested one of his elbows on an overhead beam as he balanced his hunched frame. Her flashlight's gleam pooled on his face, showing off a steely strength softened by the hint of tender pain deep in his amber eyes. Was that what drew women to him? That double-edged sword of masculinity and vulnerability? Did they imagine they could heal him?

"I was trying to get this lock open to see if these cabinets hold Armand's genealogy research." Christi jiggled the drawer. She could not dwell on her reawakening feelings for Daniel, not when things were still so unsettled between them, not when she couldn't be sure any future was possible. She'd hurt him when she'd tried to break off their engagement. Then when worry had crazed his face, she'd crumpled like a paper bag and reagreed to the engagement as long as it was open-ended.

"It's probably just his business records," Daniel said.

"Well, I won't know until I open them, will I?" Why was she so touchy?

"Allow me." With a hand on her shoulder, he gently pushed her aside to get a clear view of the stubborn lock.

She slanted him a doubtful look. "You know how to pick a lock?"

"Don't look so surprised. I'm a man of many talents." He hiked an indifferent shrug of shoulder and took the flashlight from her. "I tend to misplace my keys. Learning to pick my front door lock was a matter of survival."

And she was coming to learn, Daniel was very good at sacrificing for survival. That he'd done it for her, for the child he didn't know he'd fathered, weighed heavily on her conscience. She wished she could give him what he wanted. She wished she could take what she still desired. Mostly she wished none of the heartaches had had to happen.

"What are you using to tumble the lock?" he asked.

Christi handed him her earring. He looked at it and his smile had a curious tilt. "Give me the other."

Hands free of flashlight and improvised burglary tools, she didn't know what to do with them. They plunged inside her pocket and wrapped around a roll of antacid. "Were you following me?"

"No, Marguerite wanted a bottle of wine for her coq au vin." He gave her the flashlight and nodded toward the lock. "Point the light at the lock."

His hands hid the work of his nimble fingers, but the pad of his fingertips against the metal had her thinking of the magic of his touch. She squirmed as if a ghost had skimmed its palm along her shoulders.

"Hold the light steady."

"You've been in this basement before?" Of course

he had. *Stupid question, Christi. He has a key to the house.*

"Many times."

"Why didn't you mention the cabinets before? I could have had the riddle of Armand's genealogy solved days ago."

"I didn't know about them until I heard you rummaging under the stairs. Exploring dark, damp basements is not my idea of fun. And when I was a kid, the cabinets weren't here."

The lock gave a groan as if a beast were being set free. Then came a click—almost as a postscript. "Here you go." The drawer squealed along its tracks, hinged like the cry of an infant in pain. He bowed grandly and offered her access to the yellowing files.

"Wow! Look at them all!" The files were packed hard into the drawer. When she tried to slip one out, half a dozen tagged along. Daniel was right. These files were Armand's records of adoptions. Each folder held a record of the mother's history—medical and personal—along with the name of the adoptive family and the financial expression of their desire to own a child.

"I can't believe how many adoptions he transacted. There are at least one hundred files in this drawer alone."

"No, look. He has other cases mixed in." He was too close, and a rush of heat spread through her so fast she thought it might leap out her fingers and ignite all this brittle paper. "Here's a divorce. A custody battle. An estate settlement. They're in alphabetical order by client name."

"Can you pick the other locks for me?" she asked, partly to gain some breathing space.

"Anything for you."

The warm keel of his smile had her stomach flip-flopping like a rag in a washing machine.

The second cabinet was no different than the first. So was the third. She was about to close the drawer, when a name caught her attention. "Daniel, look!"

Langelier, Marie Marguerite was scrawled by hand across the tab. It was the only file titled in longhand. Christi had her fingers on the file, ready to extract it for a closer inspection, when the plod of Marguerite's footsteps made the stairs groan.

"Daniel?" Marguerite's strident voice called.

Christi froze. Marguerite couldn't find them going through the files. She'd surely report the misdeed to Armand, then Christi would lose her shot at the truth. Daniel's arms folded around her and spun her into the tight corner behind the file cabinets.

"Daniel?" Marguerite paused at the bottom of the stairs and looked in all directions, then mumbled in French, "If you want something done, you have to do it yourself."

Christi tried to ease out of Daniel's hold. He pulled her back, surrounding her like armor.

Rising on her toes, Marguerite reached above the wine cellar door on the rounded lip of the door frame. After she'd selected the bottle she wanted, she re-locked the door and headed back toward the stairs. Halfway there, she stopped, lurched forward on her toes, then pitched back on her heels like a wind-up toy that had run out of roll. She set the bottle of wine firmly into the dirt floor and headed to a shelf directly across from where Christi and Daniel huddled.

Christi's heart climbed halfway up her throat before she could swallow it down. Her brain frantically concocted a story to hide her presence here. One hand cradled her rebelling stomach, the other covered her mouth. To make matters worse, Daniel's body was pressed so close to hers, chest to hip, thigh to thigh, that every fiber of her being ached with awareness of his proximity, his heat, his desire. His woodsy scent stirred the memory of the pine freshener in his beat-up Mustang and the long evenings spent there snuggling and stargazing. The tiny puffs of his breath against her neck whirled her back to the alley behind the ice-cream parlor and the stolen kisses they'd shared in the dark. *Don't go there, Christi.*

Marguerite reached for a box on a high shelf. It tumbled down from the stack and landed a foot from their hiding spot. Christi caged her breath. Marguerite picked up the box, dusted the cover, and reached inside. From the mound of blue tissue paper, she extracted a rag doll.

Even in the dim hatches of light, the exquisite attention to detail on the old-fashioned doll came through. The black dress was expertly tailored. The brown hair was perfectly curled in fat boudins around a neatly embroidered face. The leather boots on the doll's feet had tiny pearl buttons.

Marguerite lovingly fingered the petticoat lace. The brimming tears magnified her huge eyes. *"Pauvre petite Amélie."*

She pressed the doll to her heart and her big body shuddered with a sigh that seemed to hold a world of wistfulness. Clutching the doll in her left arm, she placed the cover on the box and shoved it back on the shelf. A small plastic container fell, bounced off the dirt floor and rolled and rattled toward the file cabinets. As Marguerite bent to pick it up, the half-closed file drawer caught her attention. She stooped to study the file sticking out by one corner. The air became still, thick like blood, spiked with murder. Roaring, she yanked the file out of the drawer. She rose and slammed the drawer shut with her foot. Eyes ablaze, nose sniffing the air like a starved lioness who scented prey, she peered all around the dim corners of the room.

"Daniel?" The tone of her voice could have added a layer of rime to hell.

Christi reared back with a small indrawn gasp. Daniel's arms tightened around her and shrank them both deeper into the corner.

With one last fiendish look, Marguerite lumbered back up the stair with the doll and the bottle of wine. When she reached the top of the stairs, she switched the light out and slammed the door, plunging the basement in total darkness.

"Who's Amélie?" Christi asked, trying to calm the clanging of her heart and disengage herself from the prison of Daniel's arms.

"I don't know." He grabbed her flashlight and went to turn the light back on.

She flicked on the flashlight and picked up the plastic container that had lured Marguerite to the file cabinet. Through the yellowed plastic, a hundred buttons, like dead eyes, stared back at her. "What do you suppose was in that file?"

"I don't know."

Frowning she thought back to the doll. Handmade. With love. By Marguerite? "Do you suppose she had a baby and gave it up for adoption?"

"I think she'd have kept the child. My father couldn't keep a secret if his life depended on it, and

I never heard him mention that Marguerite had a child.''

She couldn't shake the heart-shaped mouth, the lace, the pearl buttons. "But in those days a child born out of wedlock was unacceptable. What if the father didn't want to marry her? Or couldn't?''

"Does it really matter, Christiane?''

"I don't know. Maybe it does.'' Marguerite seemed to wear bitterness the way her mother had worn fear. It was a cloak that was as much part of her as the color of her eyes. "It all depends what importance Armand placed on the situation. If his sister's condition could affect his position, then maybe—''

"He'd try to fix it.''

The cold fingers of anxiety stirred the acid in her stomach. What could cause such single-minded, dark focus in a man? Was it the blow of a single event that had bent him? Or the hammer of repeated insults? "Can you open the last two locks for me?''

Daniel did his trick with the earrings and the locks popped open. Armand's genealogy research remained absent. The last drawer almost flew out of Christiane's hand. She landed with a thud against him. "Easy, *trésor.*''

The drawer was empty except for a fat accordion file. Christiane balanced it on her knees and simply stared at the C.R.L. penned in black felt marker.

"What does it say?'' Daniel asked, trying to peer over her shoulder.

She fingered the letters. Sadness stroked her feather-light and razor-sharp. "It's about my mother.''

The elastic band surrounding the file snapped into

two as she stretched it. There were three sections inside the file. The thickest was labeled "Caroline." The middle section, "Christiane." And the last section, "Rosane."

"Oh." Her pulse skittered, fear a snake squirming through her gut.

Caroline's section held a long list of addresses. Here and there, notes were scribbled about some of the locations where Caroline had lived. In her dry mouth, her tongue ripped away from her palate like the duct tape her father favored for home repairs. "He's been tracking Mom ever since she left home. Always a step behind until we got to Fort Worth. We stayed there too long. No wonder she never mentioned her family. No wonder she seemed so relieved when we moved to a new place. No wonder her history was a closed subject."

As she reached into the next section, her fingers shook. There, she found information on her own milestones—schools attended, her first communion, her confirmation, her high school graduation, her daughter's birth, her college graduation, her jobs.

As if someone had whacked the back of her knees, they gave away. She sank to the ground. Daniel followed her, easing her against the solid breadth of his body. She reached into the next section and Rosane's life spilled out before her. "I never realized he kept such close tabs on us. How did he do it?"

"He had a lot of people working for him." Daniel stamped a kiss against her temple. She leaned into his solid warmth. "Not all of his adoptions went to Canadian families. Some made their way to the States."

As she was about to stuff the papers back into the

file, a crumpled document caught her attention. She unfolded it. Her jaw dropped open.

"What is it?" Daniel asked, his voice sounding as if it were underwater.

When she couldn't find her breath to answer, he reached for the sheets. The ridges of the puckered papers slipped through the boneless grip of her fingers. "A plan for the perfect murder."

Chapter Nine

Christi's ice-bound fingers made the file on her knee chatter. In black and white Armand had outlined his meticulous plans for her parents' murder.

He'd hired a terminally ill patient who wanted to die before he became incapacitated and who wanted to leave his family without any debt. In exchange for driving into her mother's car with deadly impact, Armand would deposit a million dollars into a trust account for the man's family. Had he? Had the man's family made Armand keep his end of the bargain? Or had he simply used the desperate slob to get what he wanted and reneged on his promise? She couldn't wrap her mind around such premeditated evil. How many families had he torn apart to get what he wanted?

Armand had carefully detailed Caroline's routine, down to the time she and her father would cross a busy intersection notorious for its accident rate. A note in Armand's spiky handwriting chronicled that the killer had lost his nerve and gotten inebriated before he carried out his suicide mission. The deaths were ruled an accident at the hands of a drunk driver and the police couldn't charge a dead man with anything. The man was just another drunk who'd taken two innocent lives with his own. A tragedy.

Case closed. Statistics filed. The perfect murder.

Murder.

Deliberate and intentional.

He'd killed her mother and father. He'd ripped her world apart and pretended to sew back the ragged edges with his charm and his stories and the doled out pieces of the past she was so desperate to fit together.

Liar, thief, murderer!

A sharp stab of pain gored through her. Tears zigzagged down her cheeks. A tide of acid sloshed through her stomach. "He did it after all. He killed her. Just as she'd feared all those years."

Daniel shoved the paper in the file and the file into the cabinet. With a kick he slammed the drawer shut. Then he lifted her up off the cold, dirty ground by both elbows. "You're packing your bags right now, and you're coming home with me."

"I can't, Daniel."

"Why not?"

"If Armand wants me to take my mother's place, he'll follow me to your home. If he thinks I know nothing of his plans, then I stand a better chance to deflect his attack."

In the glow of the basement's murky light, Daniel's dark eyes were the picture of implacable ferocity. "And if you fail? What about Rosane? Don't you care about her welfare?"

"I care." More than anything. She'd focused all of her energy on Rosane and her needs for the past nine years. She wasn't going to let anyone take her daughter away from her. And she would, as she'd always done, try to make her world a safe one. "She's extremely difficult right now. She's confused about who you are, the lies I told her and her place in both our lives. Moving in with you would only make things worse for her. It would tell her that I don't care about her feelings. She feels safe here. Armand wants me. He won't hurt her."

Daniel's strong hands framed her face. His thumbs smeared the tears on her cheeks. His eyes burned with the fierceness of the emotions he could barely control. "Unless it's to get to you. You saw what he did to your parents to get to you. Do you want to end up like them? Do you want your daughter?"

Her mind conjured up the sound of metal crumpling metal. It evoked the acrid stench of fire devouring the crunched hulls of cars. It brought back the stark image of the closed caskets that held the charred remains of her parents. And then she imagined Armand's satisfaction at the news that, after all these years, he'd achieved his desired end. Caroline was dead and her daughter was his for the plucking.

She couldn't let him win. She had to see this through. "Then we'll both have to make sure he can't use her."

Christi ripped herself away from the safety of Daniel's hold and flashed the beam of her light at the stacked shelves. "In the meantime, we need to look through all these boxes and find Armand's genealogy. Are you in or are you out?"

Anger galvanized every muscle of his body, and its electric wake nearly bowled her over. The sound of each of her exhalations and inhalations spurted and sighed against the corrugated surfaces of cardboard and metal like the laments of imprisoned spirits.

Would he, in his disgust with her stubbornness, leave her in this cold, dark place alone?

"In."

Her stale breath hissed out. "I'll start at this end."

An hour later, Christi lifted the cover off a box that had once contained reams of paper. The stirring of dust made her sneeze. The box now held two massive black binders and a well-worn leather book the size and heft of a diary. She hoisted one of the binders into her lap. Here it was, spread out before her, the lines that sketched her past, the webs of Armand's obsession. That was the point of this search, of course. But the truth proved much worse than any nightmare. The gaping hole between Rose and her descendants was ignored and filled with suppositions not backed with documentary proof as was the rest of the genealogy.

Then she skimmed the leather book, not a diary, but a tome of prayers to a dark prince. Armand was not functioning on the same plane of reality. In his world, the dead meant more than the living. And like a combination lock whose last number finally tumbled into place, something clicked.

"When did my mother disappear?"

"I don't know."

Marguerite would know. But Christi didn't have to ask. She could feel it in the cold hollow of her bones. Mardi Gras. Midnight. Just like Rose Latulippe.

He would strike then. She would remove the only threat he could use against her. Then she would face him. And win.

"Okay," she said, closing the box and shoving it back on the shelf. "We'll go home with you."

CHRISTI'S FIRST IMPRESSION of Daniel's condo was that it rivaled Armand's for coldness. The door opened to a bare tiled entryway with a view of the living room. The room was decorated in an impersonal theme of glass, chrome and leather. The way everything matched, a professional had to have done the decorating. Dust, like powdered sugar, iced the furniture. It looked as if no one had used the room in months.

He showed them the layout of the condo. She and Rosane would share the guest room. He set up a cot for Rosane. Then he ordered take-out Chinese, waited for the delivery and left for a rehearsal at the theater without sharing the meal with them. Between his silence and Rosane's balkiness, Christi didn't have much of an appetite and ended up storing most of the boxes full in the refrigerator.

Daniel didn't return until the red numbers on the clock in her room had clicked past two in the morning. She heard him pause before the door to their bedroom, then head back down the stairs, and could not have said why the lonesome echo of his footsteps brought her to the edge of tears.

SATURDAY DAWNED gray and heavy. Christi had a hard time separating herself from the scratchy bits of dreams that still clawed at her mind. She yawned, stretched and sighed. Today was her twenty-eighth birthday. The thought left her as gloomy as the day outside her window and the ice blue of the walls in the room.

A glance at the cot beside her bed showed her Rosane was still asleep, her back turned to her. Still angry.

Nine years ago, she'd become pregnant with Rosane. She'd grown up since then. She'd had to. Rosane and her welfare had to take center stage. Even if it meant Rosane would hate her for a while.

And Daniel?

She blew out a burst of frustrated air. What was it about him that still drew her to him? Love? Regret? The stupid fantasy she'd woven for her and Rosane?

She rolled over and punched her pillow in a vain attempt to dissipate the anxiety winding itself like a boa through her. Love knew no logic. He'd once made her believe he was as steady as the moon she tracked every night—no matter what continent her bed happened to find itself on. She'd believed him. Maybe part of her still did. Maybe that was why no other man had ever measured up to Daniel. Why she'd never let anyone get close to her after he'd left. For her, there was no one else, because in spite of everything that had happened, she could still hear the music of his soul—and it was beautiful.

Twisting to face the ceiling, she toyed with the idea of wasting the day away in bed, sweeping the past week with luscious dreams of the cheery plays she could usually conjure up at will. Perfect characters who said the perfect things at the perfect time. No roller-coaster emotions, no diabolic plot to unravel, no stubborn child to appease. Just a sweet play with a happy ending.

But it wouldn't come. All she saw when she closed her eyes was Armand and Daniel and Rosane glaring at her, each wanting something she could not give. No, this wouldn't do. She opened her eyes and stared at the stark white ceiling, but found no answers in the

Braille of stucco bumps. No use staying in bed if ghost stories were the only show.

After a quick shower to clear the remaining cobwebs from her mind, Christi returned to her bedroom to find a gold envelope propped against the door. She juggled her brush and toiletry bag so she could read the card inside. It held an invitation to her and Rosane from Daniel to have dinner with him at L'Astral tonight to celebrate her birthday.

He'd remembered.

Her throat was full of tears and a smile stretched her face.

She entered the bedroom to find Rosane sitting on the bed, phone in her lap. "Hi, Rosie. Did you sleep well last night?"

"Fine." Rosane busied herself with the buttons on a doll's dress.

Gut twisting, Christi decided to ignore the cold edge in Rosane's voice. "Where did you get that doll?"

"Marguerite gave it to me. Her name is Amélie. Isn't she pretty? Marguerite made it herself."

"Yes, she's lovely." Shivering in spite of the heat pouring from the registers, Christi laid her brush and Daniel's invitation on the dresser and picked out fresh clothes from her suitcase. Why had Marguerite given the doll to Rosane when it seemed to hold such an emotional punch for her?

Rosane's face pruned as she fidgeted with the doll's hair.

Christi fumbled through her suitcase for socks, then sat on the bed next to Rosane. How close would Rosane allow her? "Is anything on your mind?"

"No." Her shrug could have moved a mountain. "I just wanted to wish you a happy birthday."

"Thanks, honey." Christi hugged Rosane, but Rosane shirked away from the embrace. "I'd like to spend some time with you today."

"Well, Isabelle asked me to go sledding with her."

"Oh." An awkward silence fell between them. Christi slipped on her socks, then peered under the bed for her sneakers. "Daniel invited us to dinner tonight."

"I can't. Isabelle invited me to sleep over at her house tonight."

Christi looked up from the dark abyss beneath the bed to her daughter. "And who gave you permission?"

"Can I?"

The smirk on Rosane's face fueled Christi's anger. She forced herself to count to ten before she answered. "I want you to come to dinner with me. It can be my birthday present from you."

"If I go to dinner, can I sleep over at Isabelle's?"

At least Rosane had found a friend in this nightmare. Maybe time in neutral territory would do her good. She'd reacted to her forced evacuation to Daniel's condo as badly as Christi had feared. Francine Beaulieu seemed like a nice person and Isabelle the kind of friend Christi approved of. "Yes, that would be fine."

Rosane jumped off the bed. "What time is this stupid dinner?"

"Seven. And I expect you to be polite and wear a smile."

"Nothing else?"

Christi turned to Rosane and scowled at her. She

knew Rosane was trying to provoke her. "Don't push it, young lady."

"Can I go watch TV?"

"Until I find my shoes."

Rosane left, making sure to slam the door with just enough force to let Christi know how disenchanted she was with the prospect of having dinner with Daniel.

After Rosane left, Christi flopped backwards on the bed with a groan. *What am I going to do with this child?*

Soft wool tickled her fingers. She looked up to find that Rosane had left the doll sprawled on the pillow. She sat up, picked up the doll and examined it closely. Under the fine clothes, on the chest, was a red heart. In the middle, embroidered in white, was written, *Amélie, 23 sept. 1976.*

So much love was poured into the making of this doll. She could see it in every stitch. Marguerite's hard exterior suddenly made sense. This was no ordinary doll. Without doubt Christi knew that somewhere in this world there existed a woman who was born Amélie Langelier.

L'ASTRAL REVOLVED atop the Concorde Hotel, six hundred feet above sea level. From her guidebook, Christi learned that L'Astral was renowned for its European cuisine and its incredible view, and that it took an hour and a half for the restaurant to revolve the full three hundred and sixty degrees.

As they stepped off the elevator, Christi heard gasps of recognition and excited whispers in the crowded waiting area before the restaurant. Rosane clutched her hand tightly. She squeezed it back in reassurance. The maître d' looked up from his reservation book to see what the fuss was about and rushed over to them.

"Monsieur Moreau. Your table is ready," he said in very proper French.

The public Daniel and the private Daniel were very different. In that respect, he was like her. The public face was bright, gracious and downright flirtatious at times. But there was an invisible line that said, "I'll flirt with you, sign an autograph for you, but don't touch." Even his most ardent fans seemed to know not to cross that line. She sensed he'd prefer to concentrate on his music and let someone else deal with the public.

She had to admit that Daniel cut a dashing figure in his tailored charcoal suit. And he wore confidence with the same casualness he wore his clothes. It had women staring after him, naked admiration on their faces, and men wondering how they could imitate his compelling presence.

Christi wore the same dove-gray dress she'd worn at Madame Bernier's party. Knowing she was being judged with every step she took, she was glad for the good fit. She could hear whispers as she followed the maître d' down the narrow aisle between tables. "Who is that with Daniel Moreau? Wish I was her."

The maître d' seated them at a table by one of the floor-to-ceiling rounded panes of glass. Rosane chose the chair closest to the window. The night sky, littered with stars, seemed only an arm's length away. Below them, the city lights twinkled against the night-blanketed snow. The guidebook hadn't exaggerated. The view *was* breathtaking. The St. Lawrence River was a dark ribbon among the festive lights. She recognized the Château Frontenac and a few of the buildings in the old part of the city. The maître d' shooed away an autograph seeker, then assured them they would be well taken care of, bowed and left.

All around them people stared and whispered. She leaned toward Daniel across the table. "I'd forgotten you were a celebrity."

"Good." His smile spread to his eyes and made them shine that warm brandy that made her feel boneless. She could spend a lifetime getting lost in the curve of that smile, in the depth of those eyes. "This evening is for you. I thought you'd enjoy the view."

"It's beautiful."

Daniel snapped open a menu, but settled his attention on his daughter. "What do you think of the view, Rosane?"

She shrugged and looked at the other diners instead. "It's okay."

"That's a very pretty dress you're wearing. Green suits you."

"Mom made me wear it." She started kicking the chair leg with the heel of one shoe. Christi put a restraining hand on Rosane's leg and shot her a warning glance.

Daniel offered Rosane a roll from the basket in the center of the table. She pretended not to see and played instead with the charms on the bracelet she'd borrowed from Christi. He plucked a roll from the basket. "How have you been enjoying your vacation so far?"

"What do you care?"

"Rosane!" Christi turned to Daniel. "I'm sorry, she's not usually this way."

"It's all right. We all have our bad days."

"No it's not all right," Christi said. "Manners are never out of style."

"Your mother is right. It's her birthday. Let's try to make this an enjoyable meal for her, okay?"

Rosane glared at him, but didn't answer.

Frowning, he buttered his bread with the same caged precision with which she'd seen him play the piano on that first day in Quebec. "I do care. I always have."

Daniel scanned the menu and Christi followed suit. Her stomach rumbled a storm of protest. She pressed one fist into her belly. Daniel was going out of his way to repair the frayed bonds between them. She *was* going to enjoy this evening.

A waiter appeared pen and pad in hand. "My name is Yves. Are you ready to order or do you need a few more moments?"

Rosane settled on the filet mignon. Daniel chose the rack of lamb. Christi ordered a chicken dish, but the atmosphere was already so tense, she didn't think she could eat.

Maybe if she kept the conversation casual and ignored Rosane's petulance, the evening would pass by quickly enough. She twirled the stem of her water glass. "Are you all set for your concert on Tuesday?"

"Almost." Daniel seemed glad enough to follow her lead. "I have a rehearsal scheduled for tomorrow. I've reserved a seat for you and Rosane."

Before Christi could reply, Rosane started kicking the table leg and the water in the glasses spilled over their rims.

"That's quite enough, young lady!" Christi mopped the water on the tablecloth with her napkin.

"Can we go home now?"

"We haven't eaten yet. You promised to be good. It's my birthday present, remember?"

Christi was relieved when the waiter approached with their meals. She forced herself to eat, but tasted nothing as each bite fell like leaden balls into the acid soup in her stomach. Daniel attacked his meal with excessive intentness. Rosane sawed at her meat like a lumberjack.

"Your father was bad," Rosane blurted, chewing on the piece of meat she'd just placed in her mouth.

Christi and Daniel both stopped, forks in midair, and stared at each other questioningly before turning to Rosane.

Daniel set his fork down, laced his fingers and rested his forearms on the edge of the table. A tendon along his jaw twitched. "What do you mean?"

Rosane sipped water and ignored Daniel's question. Christi's stomach churned in the coiled silence.

"Rosie…" Trying to keep her temper in check, Christi spoke slowly. "What are you talking about?"

"His father was a bad man." Rosane stabbed her fork into a chunk of meat. "He did bad things."

"Who told you that? What kind of things?"

Rosane shrugged and drew a pattern in the sauce on her plate with a baby carrot. The clinks and clanks of forks and knives, the rustle of linen napkins and tablecloths, the drone of conversations with their punctuating barks of laughter hissed, hummed and hovered like a maddened hive poised to swarm.

"If someone has accused my…family of something," Daniel said without a trace of emotion, "I have a right to set the record straight, don't you think?"

Rosane glared at him. "Nobody told me. I've got

eyes. I can see.'' With her fork, she razed a ragged road through the elegant mound of whipped potatoes. ''I don't need a father.''

''Rosane…''

The knocking of toes and heels against table and chair set the glasses shaking. Christi put a hand on Rosane's leg to stop it.

Rosane whirled to face Christi. Her hand flew up. The charms on the bracelet jingled madly. Her fork cracked against the glass, crazing a lightning streak that ran from lip to base. Water dribbled from the crack. ''You lied to me!''

''About what?''

''He doesn't want me.'' Huge tears brimmed Rosane's eyes, crested and rolled down her cheeks. ''He never wanted me.''

''Rosie, we've been through this.''

Daniel pulled a handkerchief out of his pocket and handed it to Rosane. She shoved his hand aside. Christi took the handkerchief from Daniel and wiped Rosane's tears.

''Rosie, honey, please tell me where you heard these things.'' Christi kept her voice even and soothing.

''His father gave away his kids and he's—'' She hiccupped. ''He's going to give me away, too, after you're married. I don't want him to live with us, Mom. I just want you. Like it was before. Can we go? Please?''

Rosane bolted from her chair. The tablecloth caught the bracelet at her wrist. She tugged it free, knocking over all the glasses. Glass shards decorated their water-soaked meals. She shot from the table, slamming into a waiter. His tray wavered and crashed to the floor. Conversations ceased. All eyes turned toward the spectacle. The maître d' and several bus-boys rushed to clear the mess.

Cold, greasy anxiety clogged Christi's gut as she went after Rosane. She wound her arms around her daughter and led her out of the restaurant. People murmured and pointed. Armand. He was responsible for this. Who else would have anything to gain by telling Rosane such lies? Lies couched in truth. Daniel was Rosane's father. She couldn't deny that. And so the rest would sound like the truth. The acid in her stomach spun into a tornado of activity.

Stroking Rosane's back, she punched the elevator button. Daniel joined them. His face was blank as he ushered them into the elevator car. When the doors slid open in the lobby, a flash exploded in their faces. Daniel grabbed the photographer. He jerked away the photographer's camera, yanked out the roll and exposed the film, then handed both back to the young man.

Shaking, Rosane shriveled against Christi as they stood by the elevator door. ''See, Mom. I told you,'' Rosane said loudly enough for Daniel and the press to hear. ''He's bad, just like his dad.''

Chapter Ten

In the rearview mirror, Daniel spied Rosane curled into a tight ball—as far away from him as she could get in the tiny rear seat of his Porsche. She buried her head in her knees, and she sniffled, her thin shoulders trembling.

Acting like a Neanderthal wasn't his usual modus operandi. He was a public figure and having his picture snapped by opportunistic photographers was part of his life. The lies and the bits of truth spewed by Rosane had hit too close to home. The flash in his face as he stepped off the elevator had been the proverbial backbreaking straw.

The anger was still there. Millimeter by millimeter the tetanic pressure of it contracted his muscles and he ground his teeth.

He doesn't want me. He never wanted me.

The hatred vibrating in Rosane's voice echoed in his mind, shattered his heart.

The headlights cut across the hard face of night, slashing a path along the black pavement. Heat poured out of the vents, but didn't warm his icy hands. His grip choked the steering wheel. He'd *wanted* to be part of his daughter's life. It hadn't been possible. He'd needed to keep her safe from the dark stain of his world. And he'd thought staying away was the only way to achieve that goal.

He ventured a sideways glance at Christiane. Her usually expressive face was too ashen. He'd never seen her look so sick. He wished he'd stuck to his original plan of dinner at his condo. But he'd thought a neutral setting would lift their gloomy mood. And he'd wanted to impress Christiane, impress his daughter. He'd wanted to show them, what? That he was worthy?

Not his most brilliant move.

He cranked the radio on, then snapped it right off when the hot licks of jazz grated on his raw nerves. Music wasn't going to help.

The tabloids were going to have a field day with what had happened. Not that he cared; he was used to it. But Christiane wasn't and the half-truths they'd print would hurt her.

The car idled at a red light. He wasn't going to let Armand win. Not this time. He'd find a way to make Rosane believe she'd always occupied a big part of his heart, that she'd never been far from his thoughts.

The instant the light flicked to green, Daniel knew what he had to do. His pulse jitterbugged as he turned into his driveway. Would she understand?

"No, don't stop here!" Rosane shrieked from the back seat. "You promised, Mom. You promised I could sleep over at Isabelle's!"

Christiane strained against the seat belt to look at Rosane. "That was before the incident at the restaurant. We need to talk about what happened."

"I don't want to. I want to go to Isabelle's!"

"Maybe it's not such a bad idea," Daniel said, as

the engine idled and exhaust plumed from the tailpipe. He needed to talk to Christiane, to explain what his daughter would soon know. ''Being with a friend might be the best thing for her right now.''

A blast of wind squalled along the snowbank and skittered icy crystals across the windshield. In the yellow glow of the lamppost, sorrow seemed to shroud her delicate features and worry to pinch her eyes. ''She'll be safe there.''

With a nod, Christiane turned away from them both and stared at the funnels of icy flakes that drifted across his front yard like a host of tiny spirits.

''Wait here for a minute.'' He sprinted into his condo and came back out a few moments later, bearing a padded envelope he handed to his daughter. Would Rosane understand? Would Christiane forgive him? ''For you. When you're alone.''

THE FRONT DOOR of the Beaulieu's home flew open and Isabelle jumped up and down, red pigtails bouncing as she waved excitedly at Rosane. Christi made introductions. Francine Beaulieu was delighted to meet Daniel Moreau in person and blushed when she shook his hand. She smoothed her strawberry-blond hair into place and, as she talked to Christi, her green eyes kept drifting back to Daniel. Francine assured Christiane that having Rosane over wasn't an imposition and that the girls would have fun together.

''Could you make sure Rosane doesn't go to the Langeliers' on her own?'' Christi asked, wanting to ensure Rosane safety against Armand's obsession.

Francine's forehead pleated. ''Oh?''

''Armand isn't feeling well,'' Christi lied, twisting her gloves in her hand. ''A bit of a cold. I don't want her to bother him. I'll collect her first thing in the morning.''

''Of course.''

Fifteen minutes later, she and Daniel were back at his condo. Daniel threw both their coats and his suit jacket onto the back of a leather recliner. He headed straight downstairs. She had questions she wasn't sure how to ask, so she followed him to his studio. The heart of his home.

This room, too, was decorated in glass, chrome and leather, but unlike the others, it breathed life. Daniel's energy vibrated from every corner. Tapes and sheets of music were strewn over the desk against the back wall. More music was piled on top of the piano in the middle of the room. The remnants of his congealed breakfast sat on the coffee table near the stairs. On the wall above his desk hung framed reproductions of the cover art for his first six albums. The leather couch had a crumpled blue and white afghan in one corner and the large accent pillow at the other end still bore the imprint of his head.

Daniel flipped on several lights and dialed up the heat. ''It'll warm up in a minute.'' Then he took the stairs two-by-two and left her standing by the wall of glassed-in shelves.

She'd never seen so much audio equipment in one place—not even at the television station where she worked. In the midst of all this impersonal equipment, it was the black-lacquered piano that drew her. She walked to it and ran her hands over the keys, polished to a shine from use. How many hours had Daniel spent sitting on this bench absorbed in his music?

She was crazy to stay here. She should have insisted on talking with Rosane. She should simply walk upstairs and close herself in the guest room. Instead, she counted the keys on the piano, and her mind drifted to the past, to the night they'd spent under the stars.

She'd learned the outline of every muscle on his body, the heady taste of his skin, the intoxicating scent of lovemaking.

The next day, he was gone.

Nine years later, tears still choked her throat at the memory.

"Are you all right?" Daniel asked as he handed her a glass of wine.

"Uh, yes. Fine."

"Rosane is safe."

"I know." She accepted the glass, then started to give it back to him. "I can't. My stomach."

"It's nonalcoholic." There was that smile again, the one that made her heart skip beats. The room grew warmer. How high had Daniel set the thermostat?

He placed his glass on the coffee table and sidled beside her on the piano bench. "Do you play?"

"No." She was intensely aware of his body next to hers, of the heat he generated, of the tension that lined each of his muscles. "I don't know the first thing about music."

"It's simple, really." He poised his hands over the keys. Beautiful, sculpted hands. Art in themselves. "Music doesn't ask to be understood. It only asks that you open your heart and feel its texture." His fingers danced over the keys, and it was as if he'd stroked every vertebra along her spine. "Let music slide over the chords of your emotions as you drink in its sensual appeal."

Her throat was dry, so she cleared it. When that

didn't help, she sipped the nonalcoholic wine, and it tasted like unsweetened grape juice. "Isn't that a lot to ask from eighty-eight keys?"

He chuckled. "I thought you didn't know anything about music?"

"I counted them while you were upstairs."

The light generated by the two table lamps etched his profile with the passion and drive that were a living force in him. "The keys aren't the music. The notes, the space between the notes are. Music is in the soul and your reaction to music is simply a recognition of truth. Strike the right chord and you'll find the desired emotion."

"It sounds so...calculated."

He shrugged. "It is. And it isn't."

"I always thought music was magic." Christi set her glass aside, then wished she hadn't because her hands no longer had anything to confine their restlessness.

"A chemist experiments with chemicals. He mixes them and observes what happens. I do the same with notes."

"No magic?" she teased.

Half his mouth tipped up. "Maybe a little magic."

"When did you know you had a talent for music?" She gripped the back edge of the bench and leaned away from the charged atmosphere that seemed to crackle around him. His fingers on the keys slowed. The notes sounded like tears.

"When I was eight." His tone was casual. His shrug careless. But his eyes were full of painful ghosts. "I used to lie in my bed and hum songs to cover the sound of my parents fighting. At first they were other people's songs. Then I found mine."

She could not remember a single argument between her parents. They'd shared a silent understanding, a stalwart support, which circled them and nobody else. It was just as well they'd died together. Without the other, the one left behind would have been only half a person. Absently, she rubbed at the tightness in her throat. "What did they argue about?"

"My father's affairs." The chords Daniel banged out vibrated the room with resentment. "Rosane is right. My father wasn't a good man."

"What did she mean by 'He gave his kids away?'"

"He would seduce young girls." Daniel swallowed the bitter truth like a pill. "Then when they got pregnant, he gave them Armand's name."

And Armand sold the babies to his clients. *He gave away his kids.* A twist of the truth Armand had used to sow the seeds of mistrust. "Daniel—"

"Shh." He kept playing, painting the changing landscape of his emotions with notes. Now he plucked an intricate pattern on the keys.

"That looks complicated," she said, glad to change the subject.

"It's not. Music has five basic elements. This is melody." He seduced a love song from the piano. "Now listen." He missed one note, and she winced. "That one discordant note ruined the harmony of the piece." He thumped out a march. "This is rhythm."

He switched to a classical piece. "Tone color comes from the instrument. A violin would give this a different tone. So would a flute. An orchestra mixes tones to give a full rainbow of colors." He ended the piece with a flourish. She sighed. "That satisfied 'ah' is what form is all about." He flashed her an approving smile. "It's the wholeness, the sense of completion at the end. And when a musician mixes all the elements together, he can control the listener's mood.''

Daniel played his own music now. She recognized anger in *Fugue de Pégasse,* "Pegasus' Fugue.'' Love for a child in *Berceuse pour un Ange,* "Lullaby for an Angel.'' He plucked out joy, triumph and sorrow in pieces she didn't recognize.

Daniel paused and speared her with a look that was both steely strength and raw exposure. "This is you.''

His fingers stroked the keys with intimate care and from the first note, Christi was ensnared by the music's seductive fever. She recognized the melody as the same one that had plagued her the night of Daniel's proposal. How could that be? This was the first time she'd ever heard it. The room got smaller. Her skin prickled with ice and fire. Sweat slicked her palms. Her breath got lost somewhere between her lungs and her mouth. The music swirled around her, making her feel dizzy. Her pulse beat to the same erotic pattern as the notes. Her stomach, which should be a raging hurricane, was uncharacteristically calm. The expected fiery heat burned much lower.

When Daniel stopped playing in midstream, she felt as if he'd caressed every inch of her body and every cell pined for more.

When Daniel's gaze connected with hers, unadulterated desire blazed in the cognac of his eyes. "That's how you make me feel, Christiane.''

His voice trembled with the same tension that threatened to disintegrate her. The knuckles of his left hand skimmed her cheek. To her surprise, she didn't shatter; she yearned for more. The rising flood of desire clouded her judgment. Right now, there was only

Daniel and her aching need to wrap herself around him. Would she ever learn? "Will you be there in the morning?"

"Every morning, if you'll just let me."

He kissed her then, a slow gentle kiss that tasted of regret, of sorrow and of longing. "Give me—us—another chance, Christiane. That's all I ask."

The ice she hadn't known was caged in her thawed. She melted as rivers of pleasure flowed through her. She melted as torrents of warning bolted right behind her. She melted as he took her into his arms—to the only place she'd ever called home.

"Touch me, Daniel," she whispered against his lips, wanting the impossible, knowing it was all an illusion that would soon vanish. "I want to feel the music in your hands." One last time.

Touch me. Daniel thought he'd explode at Christiane's invitation. His muscles ached from the effort it took not to rush.

He'd imagined a perfect evening for her. Dinner would've gone smoothly. Conversation would've flowed easily. The birthday cake would've made her gasp in surprise and laugh with joy.

Yet as badly as the evening had gone, with her here, his house felt like home for the first time since he'd bought it. She still wanted him. He could feel the liquid passion in her that always reminded him of flutes and strings.

At his silence, she cocked her head, bemused. "What?"

He was staring. He couldn't help it. She was his sun, his muse, his inspiration.

Searching for the words he knew she needed, he

stood from the piano bench, taking her with him. Reason and rationality weren't going to help him tonight. Words risked misinterpretation. Words had sharp edges that wounded. Words failed. But not this. Not this sweet remembering, this seamless fit, this powerful harmony of souls. This she would understand. The words could come later.

Urging her body closer, he explored the contours of her jaw, nipped at her earlobe before descending to the long column of her neck. The leap of her pulse, the answering surge of his own, gave him a rare satisfaction. His fingers tugged at the zipper of her dress. With excruciating precision, he slid the metal grip along the teeth, trailing both thumbs down the newly exposed silk of her skin. She sighed. He trembled. This was a language they'd spoken well.

"Daniel..." Her whisper scorched his ear.

He hooked two fingers to the spaghetti strap that held her dress up and pushed the silver material off her shoulders. It slid down her body and landed in a shimmering pool around her ankles. His mouth savored the delectable cream of her skin. He drank in her scent. Both had left an imprint nine years ago and rediscovering them was like salve on a wound. "It was good between us, Christiane."

"Yes." She clawed at his shirt, trying to free its tail from the confinement of the waistband. "Let me touch you."

"It still is."

Her fingers trembled as they freed the buttons of his shirt and splayed over his chest.

His tongue teased the nipples straining at the ivory lace of her bra. As she swayed against him, his hands did as she'd pleaded earlier and touched every inch of her he could reach.

And when that was no longer enough, before his knees grew too weak, he carried her to the leather couch. Kneeling before her, watching every nuance of gray track desire across her eyes, he slowly unrolled the smoky silk of her stockings down her legs. The ivory panties quickly followed. She reached for him, grabbed his shoulders as if she were drowning and he was a lifeline. He leaned in for a kiss and released her breasts from their lacy prison.

His voice was husky as he clasped her close and tried to calm his flayed nerves. "You drive me crazy, Christiane. You always did."

"I'm glad." Her smile was a satisfied secret as she fumbled with his belt.

Daniel rid himself of his clothes, then lowered himself next to her. He found her mouth and kissed it hungrily. Her hips rocked against his, undulating in a primitive beat that thrilled through him. When she hooked one foot around his calf, opening herself to him, he could not resist the invitation. He clung to her in fierce possession, hearing only the sounds of the music they made.

It was a fugue, a flight in two voices. A manic rhythm and a strong countermelody. Irresistible. Unavoidable. Irreversible. This powerful force mounted until he was certain he would go mad. It rose in a fever pitch to a final crescendo. He spilled all of his need into her, and as she accepted him with a rhapsody of intimate embraces, he spiraled out of control.

When the room stopped spinning, he shifted his weight, so as not to crush her. Her jagged breath on his chest rasped a counterpoint to his own ragged one.

Her hand pressed against his heart kept time with his pulse. Her heartbeat rapped against his side, a snare to his timpani. This symphony of breath, of pulse, of heartbeat was the most beautiful music of all.

As he pressed a kiss to her temple, the yellow eye of the moon stared down at him through the silver slats of blinds on the window. She'd told him about the constant moves that had disoriented her, about sleeping with the curtains open and searching for the moon that had offered the only constant in her life. He'd once promised her he'd be her moon. And she'd accepted his word as truth with heart, body and soul.

Renouncing that vow was his greatest regret.

As much as he'd worked to keep history from repeating itself, he could not erase it. He was as haunted by what he hadn't done as by what he had done. And even in the midst of this perfect concert he could not forget that old sins were catching up to him.

CHRISTI AWOKE in Daniel's arms, a delicious ache like warmed honey stirring through her limbs. Her head rested comfortably in the crook of his neck. One finger played absently with the soft hair on his chest. Sometime in the night, they'd moved to his bedroom, and the morning's gloomy light, trickling through the shades, offered her a first glance.

His bedroom looked more like a through station than a place where he sought comfort. The same decorator who'd done the living room had left her cold mark on this room, too. Silver walls, navy accents, a splash of cranberry—all hard lines and uncompromising chic. A suitbag was draped over a stiff-backed chair. Several days' worth of clothes made a mound on the navy carpet. On the night table Christi spotted two silver frames. One held a picture of her. A smile bloomed when she recognized it. "You took this picture from my mother's album."

Even with sleep still snuggling at the corners of his mind, he looked sheepish. "I needed something, and your mother let me take it."

"You thought about me?" Her gaze lingered over his, searching for proof she hadn't given her heart away again for nothing.

"Every day." His voice, soft and gentle, breathed longing. He spooned against her, tasted the round of her shoulder, and stirred in her a hunger that took her by surprise. She wanted to believe.

In the other picture, Daniel stood arms draped around two women. She recognized the smaller one as his mother, Chantal. The other looked enough like him that she assumed it was his sister, Lise.

"I need to go get Rosane." She loathed to leave this haven of peace, but she couldn't linger here. Not until Armand was stopped. If she was right, she had two more days. Then she could think about Daniel, about their possible future. "I don't know what got into her last night."

Daniel's body ripped away from her back and hips like Velcro, leaving a cold yawning that felt as wide as the Grand Canyon. He got up and jammed his legs into a pair of discarded jeans. "Armand."

Shivering, she reached for the first piece of clothing she found—a navy sweatshirt imbued with Daniel's woodsy scent. "I need to talk to him, too."

"No." The sharpness of Daniel's voice left no room for compromise. "I don't want you anywhere near him."

Sitting on the edge of the bed, she ran a hand

through her hair. She didn't want to argue. Not after last night, not when she was still feeling the echo of his touch ring all over her. "I need a shower. The linen closet in the guest bath has no towels."

"They're in the master bathroom. I'll get some for you." He strode to the bathroom and came out with a pile of folded towels, cranberry and navy.

"Daniel?" Pulling the comforter across her lap, she swallowed hard. "Do you love me?"

Torment forked through his eyes as he handed her the stack of towels. "Sometimes love isn't enough."

She took them and hugged them close. "If not love, then what?"

His gaze pleaded with her. She shouldn't have let herself believe in a dream. She shouldn't have asked the question if she wasn't ready to hear the answer. He'd warned her, hadn't he? He wanted to keep their relationship on a physical level. He was afraid to love her. That she understood his fear didn't hurt any less. She watched as Daniel slipped away from her, pulling a protective steel of sadness around him. "Never mind. Don't answer." She lifted the stack of towels. "Thanks. I won't be long."

She got up too abruptly and banged her knee into the bedside table. The silver frames tottered and fell over. She picked up the frame containing the picture of his mother and sister and placed it back on the night table. "Did your sister ever make it as a doctor?"

"Yes. She's married now and lives in Montreal."

As she lifted the frame with her picture, the spidered glass tinkled to the carpet. A small rectangle fluttered out from behind the buckled picture and landed beneath the stiff skirt around the bed. "Does she have children?"

"No."

Her fingers reached under the navy pleat and clamped around the rectangle. "Then who did you write *Berceuse pour un Ange* for?"

When he didn't answer, she peered at him over her shoulder. His look was as remote as a prisoner facing execution. A sense of wrongness traversed the length of her spine.

"Christiane…" The forlornness in his voice tripped her heart, sent it spinning in a free fall.

She turned over the rectangle, knowing what she'd see. She was wrong. It was much worse. It wasn't a recent picture of his daughter, but a much older one. Rosane on the day she'd brought her home from the hospital. She wore a pink cap, a frilly one-piece suit and a sky-blue blanket. Her eyes were half-closed. Her tiny fist lay crooked against her cheek. How had he gotten this picture? "You knew." Her breath, banked low in her chest, was stale like smoke. "You knew about Rosane all along."

His hands rose and fell in a helpless gesture. "Christiane…why don't you take your shower and we'll talk later."

There was both pain and dismissal in his voice. A burning throb filled her stomach. "When did you get this picture of Rosane?"

"Christiane…"

"No, don't put me off. When did you get that picture?"

Daniel stared right at her. She'd never seen him this cold, this remote. "On her first birthday."

Gasping, she clutched her baby's picture to her

heart. Her mind reeled. He'd known. He'd known all along, and he'd never said anything. "How did you find out? When?"

"I don't want to discuss it right now."

"I do."

"Can't you leave things as they are?" Half turning away from her, he raked a hand through his sleep-tousled hair. "We had a special evening—just the two of us. We made love, Christiane, and found each other again. I want to hang on to that."

"I need—"

"I know." He came to her, lifted her to her feet. His hands ran up and down her arms. "I need last night to last a little bit longer."

A tumult of emotions passed through Daniel's eyes. He could probably go to the piano and express each one through music. But he didn't have the words to put to any of them. They came out in a choked machine-gun burst. "Armand gave me Rosane's picture on her first birthday, along with a promise to ruin all of our lives if I should ever try to see you again." He lifted his shoulders, then dropped them. "I believed him. Then it was too late."

"I—"

Shaking his head, he pushed her toward the door. "Go take your shower. We'll talk about it later."

She nodded, picked up the towels and headed for the bathroom.

Later. Everything was later with him. He'd love her later. He'd take care of Rosane later. Time was running out. Later would be too late. Why couldn't he see that?

At the sink, she doubled over when her stomach screamed a protest against the twisting tension coiling through every muscle of her body. She clutched at the offending organ, then groped her way to the toilet and vomited the meager contents of her stomach.

When she was done, she rested on the floor for a minute. Cold and quivering, she rose, rinsed her mouth and noticed a trace of blood. A piece of her soul. Still shaking, she brushed her teeth.

In the shower, she scrubbed his scent from her skin, but couldn't wipe the memory of him from her mind. She wanted to cry, but if she did, she'd never stop, and she didn't want him to know how deeply he'd hurt her.

She dressed in layers and headed down to the kitchen. The smell of coffee and the sound of a kettle boiling greeted her. Daniel stood at the open refrigerator with his back to her.

"I'm afraid all I have that's edible is frozen waffles. I'll have to call in a grocery order." He'd changed into fresh jeans and a bottle-green sweater that warmed the color of his eyes, but not their soul.

"I'm not hungry. I need to see Rosane."

He nodded. "I'll drive you."

As she grabbed her purse and headed out into the frigid morning air, she didn't trust herself to speak, and she couldn't hazard a guess as to what was going on in Daniel's head. Where to go? What to do? The answer was home. Except that she had no idea where that was anymore.

Chapter Eleven

Francine Beaulieu stared at Christi with wide eyes, an open mouth and a hand on her chest. "No, Rosane is not here. She went with Isabelle and my husband to the Flapjack Breakfast, then they will stay for the soapbox derby and for some skating with Bonhomme. Did Monsieur Langelier not tell you?"

"I haven't seen him this morning."

"I called the number you gave me and you were not there, so I called Monsieur Langelier, and he said you would not mind. He said he would let you know. They will be back this afternoon. I'm sorry. I thought—"

Christi waved Francine's guilt away. "It's fine. Really. Thank you."

"I will bring her to you as soon as she comes back." Francine reached for a bright red coat, hanging from a hook by the door. "I can go find her if—"

"No, that's fine." Christi backed away from the front door. "I'm sure the girls will have fun." Rosane was safe. That was what mattered. She would have a talk with Armand, and really, it was better if Rosane was otherwise engaged.

When Christi reached Daniel's car, she kept going. "I'll walk the rest of the way to Armand's house."

"You can't go there."

"He's shown me he's willing to use Rosane to get what he wants. She won't step foot in that house again, but I have no choice. I have to talk to him."

Daniel nodded. "I'll go with you."

"Don't you see? It's part of the game, Daniel. I have to play it Armand's way for now if I stand any chance of winning."

"I can't leave you there alone." He got into his car and headed to the gray stone house.

The snow squeaked under her heels and the cold snap of the breeze felt good on her overheated cheeks. Today was as gloomy as yesterday and the smell of moisture filled the air. Christi looked up at the sooty sky. Already a few tiny snowflakes swirled down lazily. How could she let herself fall into Daniel's arms so easily? And yet, being there had felt so right. Wasn't a seesawing mind the first sign of madness? That was it. She was definitely losing her mind. She swished her hand through the pocket of her coat, but found only shreds of wrapper littering the bottom. No antacid. Did she have any left?

Christi went through the back door of Armand's house. She crept past the kitchen. Marguerite knelt in the pantry at an odd angle as if she were searching for something just out of reach. She muttered something in French, but Christi couldn't make out the words. She half thought of asking Marguerite if she needed help, then changed her mind. She didn't want to deal with her right now.

She wanted to crawl into bed and hide until she'd sorted out her feelings. But moping was a luxury she couldn't afford right now. Certainly not here. Not with Armand and his diabolic obsession lasered on her. It was time to concentrate on important things. Like staying alive.

If her guess was right, Armand's attack would come on Tuesday. Why else would he have set the scene so carefully? He was waiting for Mardi Gras. She wasn't in any danger until then. But to foil him, she would need her senses sharp and not muddled by her own obsession with Daniel.

As she stepped into the foyer, she spotted a newspaper on the telephone table and Daniel's jacket on a chair beside it. Had he already cornered Armand? As she shrugged off her coat, the headline splashed across the front page caught her eye. *L'enfant du Diable?* The devil's child? Beneath was a picture of Rosane standing amid a chaos of broken dishes at L'Astral, her green dress splattered with raspberry sauce and white crumbs of cake from the waiter's tray. Her face was a study in anger and humiliation. The article described Rosane's extraordinary performance at the restaurant. Then it went on to speculate about Christi's pedigree and her reasons for being in Quebec City. It ended with a cryptic note that pointed to the vague resemblance between their beloved Daniel Moreau and the child. The author ended with a promise to unearth the answers to all the questions burning in his readers' minds about the two strangers.

Christi tossed the paper back on the telephone table. What had happened to her plans for a quiet vacation? Two weeks ago, a trip to Quebec City had seemed such a good idea. She would get to know her mother's family, her history, her roots. Fiery warmth flooded her stomach with renewed fervor. She shook her head and started up the stairs. *Don't think about that.*

Rosane wouldn't be back until this afternoon. She had plenty to do before then. First, she'd confront Armand about the lies he'd told Rosane. Coming after her was one thing, using her daughter quite another. Determined, she strode toward Armand's office. The black and white stripes of the wallpaper seemed to shimmer and disoriented her for a moment. On the stairs, voices floated down to her.

"Her father was an orphan," Armand said, in French. "He had no family. With Caroline dead, I am her family. When Christiane dies, I will be granted custody of Rosane."

"As the biological father, custody will revert to me," Daniel countered.

What was he saying? Custody? Of her daughter? He'd promised. She jammed a fist under her rib cage, trying to calm the wildfire burning there. Daniel couldn't be that cruel. He'd promised.

Armand pitched into a coughing fit. As she edged to the door, he spit phlegm into a handkerchief.

"A sick old man at that," Daniel said, without emotions. "No court would hand you custody of a child."

Maybe Daniel was that cold. Maybe he didn't care after all. Maybe he'd played her this time as expertly as he had nine years ago. Had his prize been Rosane all along?

Armand sat in his stiff desk chair, puffing on one of his vile cigarettes. The smoke curled, wafted in her direction and snaked down her throat. Nausea joined the fire in her stomach. All she could see of Daniel was his long outstretched legs, crossed at the ankles on the corner of Armand's desk as if he didn't have a care in the world. And here he was negotiating with the devil for his own daughter's soul.

"You're a musician," Armand said with a condescending smile. "You travel. You lead a lewd life. What kind of home could you offer a child?"

"A better one than a crazy old man."

They were discussing Rosane's custody as if she were a horse at auction, as if her own death was a matter of fact. The whole situation was so absurd; she didn't know whether to laugh or cry.

"Keep your end of the bargain, let me have Christiane, and I shall let you have your daughter."

Christi heard a gasp. When the two men turned to face her, she realized it had spouted out of her. Her hands gripped the door frame as if her life depended on it. She stared at Daniel, at his impassive face, at the casual slant of his body. He'd used her. He'd known Armand's plan all along. He was part of it. The classic distraction. Seduce the stupid girl, take what you want, then let the carcass drop where it may. And she'd fallen for the ploy, for him, not once, but twice.

Daniel rose from his chair and stretched a hand out to her. "Christiane—"

"No! Stay away from me." She backed into the hallway. Her vision wavered as if she were looking through a funhouse mirror. Racing down the stairs, she rebounded against the wall. Gripping the handrail on both sides, she pushed on. Her mind whirled. She had to get out of this house. She had to find Rosane and leave this city, this country. The only thing she'd found here was pain.

And maybe if she ran fast enough, she could leave her broken heart behind.

"CONGRATULATIONS." Daniel glared at Armand still sitting in his chair. "You got what you wanted."

Armand lifted a hand like a maestro ready to conduct an orchestra. "I told you. I always get what I want. You should know that by now."

Daniel didn't stay to debate the point. He rushed after Christiane to explain what she'd overheard. At the foot of the stairs, he grabbed the jacket he'd tossed on the chair by the telephone table and followed her through the open front door.

She'd already made good time down the sidewalk—without a coat. He cursed Armand and blamed himself. Why was it that when it came to her he could do nothing right?

Gray light steeped the morning with gloom. Snow ticked like demon nails on the nylon of his jacket. Wind lashed against him as if it were Armand's minion trying to push him away from Christiane. Was there no way to put a tourniquet on this hemorrhage from the past?

She shouldn't have come. She should have stayed home where she was safe and happy. Daniel caught up with her on the edge of Parc Champs de Bataille. His breath was a raw rasp as he gathered her in his arms. She desperately tried to wrench free, flogging his shins and shoulders with feet and fists.

"Christiane, let me explain." He suppressed a curse as the toe of her boot connected once more with his shinbone.

"You used me." Her voice ripped through the cold air like a crack of thunder.

"No. Listen—"

"Why? So you can tell me more lies?"

The forsaken look ransacking her eyes shredded his soul. "So you can hear the truth."

"It's too late." A bubble of hysteria rose from deep inside her and surfaced in an explosion of volcanic proportions. "It's too late." She shook her head. The wind writhed through her hair. Her fingers dug into his shoulders and shoved, but he held on to her elbows. "For everything."

Daniel's heart constricted with every beat. It was too late for him. But not for her. He could still save her. "I'll help you find Rosane."

"No. She's mine." Snowflakes stamped cold kisses against her cheeks, melted into tears. "Let me go."

Her skin was turning to ashes before his eyes. Her lips took on a bluish cast. The light in her eyes faded to nothing. After what she'd heard, he couldn't blame her for hating him. She wouldn't hear the truth now. He'd follow and make sure she was safe. He wouldn't breathe easy again until she was on a plane heading south. "At least take my coat."

As he shed his jacket, she took a step away from him. With a hand on her elbow, he held her in place and slipped the jacket around her shivering shoulders. "Don't be a fool. Frozen, you won't do your daughter any good."

The coat swallowed her whole. Her skin looked ghostly pale against the black nylon. Fists in his pockets, fingers curled tight, he watched her as she rushed away from him towards the old part of the city, her shoulders hunched. The wind's cold fingers pried into the wool of his sweater and pinched the breath from his lungs. Letting go was so much harder than hanging on.

She'd walked only a few meters when she doubled over and crumpled on the sidewalk.

Daniel raced to her. "Christiane?"

There was no answer but a moan. When he tried to pry away her hands from her stomach, her grasp tightened.

"Let me help you."

Then she went limp. Her skin looked translucent. Panic seized hard and fast. She couldn't die. Not now. Frantically, he felt for a pulse, but his own mad one got in the way. He placed a hand over her heart and was rewarded by a weak thump. He scooped her up in his arms, willing her to stay alive as he sprinted to his car. He strapped her in, gunned the engine, turned the heat full-blast and sped toward the hospital.

His father's ring, cold and hard against the steering wheel, caught his attention. He hurt everyone he loved. Just like his father. He clenched his jaw and pressed down on the accelerator.

"Christiane, talk to me. Come on, *trésor,* talk to me."

He'd spent years denying it. But he couldn't anymore. Not with Christiane's life ebbing before his eyes.

He was the devil's seed—his father's son in every sense of the word.

SITTING HERE in this silent hospital room, Daniel was keenly aware of the snow beating against the window, of the scent of sickness and death that even the strongest antiseptic couldn't quite mask, of the silvering of the starched sheet by the gloomy light drizzling through the window. Never had he felt so helpless as he did now, watching Christiane's still figure in bed.

She looked so close to death. Her white skin and pale blond hair held little contrast against the sheets. From the second he'd seen her at Madame Bernier's party, he'd wanted nothing but her safety. He'd let her down. He would do anything to hear the music of her laughter, see the light dancing in her eyes, feel the pulse of her life beating across the room.

The door to her room opened and a gray-haired doctor, glasses low over his nose, entered, peering down at a chart.

Daniel sprang to his feet and pumped the doctor's hand. His clenched throat relaxed. "Thank you for coming to see me. Will she be all right?"

"She has a gastric ulcer, but there's no serious bleeding. We'll keep her here for observations and a few tests. If her condition stabilizes, she can go home tomorrow. I've prescribed some stronger antacid and something that will speed up the normal healing process. She'll be fine, but she'll need to take care of herself once she's discharged." The doctor slanted him a reassuring smile and gave him a firm pat on the shoulder. "Don't worry. She'll be just fine. I'll be back later to check on her progress."

After the doctor left, Daniel resumed his watch for signs of life. He breathed with her, willing her chest to rise and fall. How could the doctor say she'd be all right when she looked so ill?

Christiane stirred in her sleep. A worried look crimped her face. Daniel scooted the chair closer to her bed, reached for her hand and stroked the cold skin. She had the dazed look of a waking child.

"What time is it?" she asked in a groggy voice.

Daniel brought her hand up to his lips and whispered a kiss across her knuckles. "It's almost two."

"Rosane." Christiane pulled her hand free and started to strip off the sheet. "I don't want her going to Armand's."

Daniel coaxed her back under the covers. "Shh. Don't worry. I called Francine. She'll keep Rosane at her home until I can pick her up later."

"No!" Panic unfurled across her face, as if he were as much a threat to her as Armand. "I don't want Rosane with you. I need to call her."

Christiane groped for the phone on the bedside table. Her hand slipped and her arm crashed into the hard edge, leaving a red mark.

Daniel propped her back up and massaged the bruising skin. "You need to take care of yourself."

Eyes wild, her fingers tightened around his hand. "I want her to stay with Francine. She'll be safe there. Promise you won't take her. Promise!"

He deserved that, but her suspicion of his motives still cut as deeply as if she'd used a knife. What she needed more than words now was reassurance. "I promise. Now rest. Doctor's orders."

Her grasp weakened and she nodded. Gently, he settled her back against the pillow and tucked the gray blanket around her. Her eyes closed, and he kissed her softly on the forehead. A dull ache filled the space where his heart should be. "I promise."

A MALEVOLENT ENERGY seeped into the room. Its presence reached out to her as Christi tried to pry herself from under the opaque blanket of drug-induced sleep. Dark like a nightmare, the distorted shape slid over the shadow-dappled surface of the floor and sat in the chair Daniel had occupied only hours ago.

Where was Daniel now? With Rosane? Where was she? Had he kept his promise? Weak, drugged and in pain, there was nothing Christi could do to protect her daughter. She shouldn't have brought her here to this bad dream. If anything happened to Rosane, Christi could never forgive herself. As soon as she was discharged, they were leaving.

The shape in the chair took on sharp edges, became a man. In the bile-colored light eking through the window, Armand's hair shone like polished shoes and his eyes seemed to glow an eerie orange. He twirled a fedora in his hands.

"You gave us quite a scare," he said genially. "How are you feeling?"

"Better." She propped herself up to a sitting position and scanned her surroundings for possible weapons.

He rose and tossed his hat on the seat of the chair, draped his coat on the back. "I brought something to cheer you up."

What? Bat's wings and eyes of newt? She didn't give him the satisfaction of an answer.

He reached into the bag at his feet and brought out a white box. He placed the box at the foot of her bed, its hard side cold against her feet even through the blanket. From the box, he extracted a red evening dress with meticulous care. "What do you think?"

"It's very pretty. I don't think it's your style though. Although red will be a pleasant change from your usual black."

A smile cracked the dry skin stretched taut over his prominent bones. "It is for you. You must wear it to

Daniel's concert. You will be the most beautiful woman there.''

I can't go. I can't sit there and listen to Daniel play. Not after last night. Besides, by Tuesday night, she'd be back in Fort Worth. She looked away from the dress.

Icicles hung from the top of the window, snake fangs dripping venom. Snowflakes plinked against the glass and crawled down its length like bloated ticks. The shadow of their squiggly tracks wriggled against her blanket as if it were covered with worms. ''I don't think I'll be well enough to attend.''

''But you must. It will be a moment of triumph for Daniel. You must share it with him.''

The brittle music of tiny fists of snow knocking at the window unraveled her nerves. ''A moment of triumph?''

''Yes. He is performing a new piece. It is magnificent. He would be very upset if you were not there.'' Armand gave her a hangdog look that seemed much too rehearsed to be genuine. ''The doctor said you would be well enough to go home in the morning. I specifically asked if the concert would be too much for you, and he said that as long as you rested and avoided stress, there was no problem with your attending.''

''How nice of you to care.'' The theater. That's where Armand planned to kill her. How did he think he could get away with murder in the middle of a crowd?

''I do.'' He draped the dress artfully over the foot of the bed. ''I care very much. I shall leave the dress here for you. Perhaps seeing something so lovely will lift your spirits. You sleep now, and I will return in the morning.''

''Don't bother.'' The hammer of her heart beat heavily, pounding blood against her brain. ''Daniel will drive me home.'' Then to the airport.

''He will be much too busy getting ready for his concert.'' Armand sat in the chair and folded his hands neatly in his lap. Slivers of ice flowed through her veins as his cold gaze pierced her. ''I always knew your daughter was more powerful than you.''

Christi bolted upright. Pain doubled her over, had her cradling her stomach. ''You leave Rosane out of this. She's just a little girl.''

Armand rose and slipped on his coat. ''Yes, *ma chère enfant,* she is just a little girl. Keep that in mind.''

''Are you threatening me?'' She gripped the sheet, ready to fling it off, launch herself across the room and shred the skin from this skeleton of a man. He would *not* touch Rosane.

''Your daughter is safe with her little friend.'' Relief warmed her icy skin. Daniel had kept his promise. But the moment of peace was fleeting. Armand placed his hat on his head. ''For now.''

He would not let her go. She saw that now. Did she really want to go through another six months, another year, of dodging his wicked moves and wondering what other sacred days he judged perfect for a sacrifice? Did she really want to imbue Rosane with the sense of fear that had chased her throughout her own childhood? Even if it took only a month for Armand to succumb to the cancer eating his lungs, it was too long.

This game had to end now.

Armand had picked the day and the place.

She knew his plan—she was forewarned.

"Okay." She shrank back into the pillow. "Whatever you want. Just tell me, and I'll do it."

His smile was triumphant. "Wear the dress. Attend the concert." He reached for the door handle. The knob moved with a scream. "And all shall end well."

ARMAND DROVE home slowly. His visit had gone quite well. The doctor was insistent about Christiane spending a few days at the hospital. But that wouldn't do at all. When he'd explained the importance of Christiane's presence at the concert, the doctor had wisely relented. Of course, his veiled threat to expose the doctor's affair to his wife hadn't hurt.

Christiane had been a little harder to sway, but he'd found the magic words to motivate her. He smiled at his reflection in the rearview mirror. Making people see his way. That was his gift. He'd failed only once. And once is all he allowed himself.

Everything would be perfect this time—as close to the actual legend as he could get. He would make his triumphant exchange at the stroke of midnight during the biggest party in town. Everyone who was anyone would witness his ascension to power—just as Rose's community had borne witness to her betrothal. Nothing, no one could stop him. Just as then, the music would entrance the crowd, keep them glued to their seats, unable to move. And once he'd gained his prize, they would forget the glory they had witnessed, just as Rose's neighbors had. Their puny brains could not comprehend such a *coup de maître*.

Keeping Daniel and Christiane apart until the concert would be simple enough now that she thought

Daniel and he were allies. Armand couldn't afford to have them conspiring this close to his triumph. The stage was set. Everything was in place. All that was left was getting Christiane out of the concert hall and into the backstage area just before midnight.

Except for the fact that he'd been denied Rosane's company, this day had been an excellent one indeed.

Armand turned into the driveway and parked in the garage. Oblivious to the cold whip of wind and the dark skin of night, he made his way to the house. Only the light above the sink threw spikes of light into the room, Marguerite had probably already retired to her suite.

He'd promised himself he would not drink tonight so he could have a clear head for the most important day of his life. But his discussion with Christiane had left his blood hot with anticipation. He licked his lips. One drink wouldn't hurt.

He headed for the basement and the wine cellar. Once there, he lit a candle, then chose a bottle of his favorite red. He uncorked it, poured himself a glass and sat in the rickety wooden chair. The familiar bouquet of the wine filled his nostrils. He savored the earthy tinge. He leaned back with a deep exhalation of pure pleasure.

Reaching into his breast pocket, he took out a photo of Caroline and propped it against the base of the silver candlestick. He took another sip of wine. "What a day I've had. It's hard to be patient when I'm so close to my goal." He raised his glass in a toast. "To success. To eternal life. And to you, *chère cousine,* for your daughter."

He reached for the bottle again and shrugged one shoulder. "I know. I said only one glass. But it would be a shame to waste a perfectly good bottle of wine. My last as a mortal man. You wouldn't begrudge this, would you, *ma belle* Caro?"

Halfway through the bottle a thought occurred to him. "I almost forgot." He went to a hollow barrel and lifted out a wooden chest. From a pocket in his vest, he extracted a key and unlocked the coffer. He reached into the velvet lining.

"Here it is." He held the knife for Caroline to see. "Recognize it? This time it will not fail me." He turned the blade and delighted at the way light kissed the polished metal, gleaming along the sharp edge like fire. With a satisfied grunt, he inserted the knife in its ceremonial sheath, placed it in his breast pocket and patted it. "The instrument of my glory."

Chapter Twelve

By the time Christi had signed all the papers and was officially discharged from the hospital, it was past noon. Knowing that Rosane was safe at Francine's, Christi had opted to return to Armand's house, rather than to Daniel's condo. She couldn't handle multiple crises at once. Not with her legs feeling like wooden stilts, her stomach like an alien growth and her head thick and mushy like a watermelon.

She'd take care of them one at a time. Armand and his obsession came first. At his home, she could keep an eye on him. Then she could unravel the rest. Dressed in a teal sweatsuit, she picked up Fumée who was twining herself around Christi's legs, purring like an outboard motor and started down the stairs. "I miss her, too," she said and hugged the kitten.

When Christi entered the kitchen, Marguerite was sitting at the table, reading a leather-bound book. A fragile china cup of coffee was all but lost in her pudgy right hand. A pot of chicken soup simmered on the stove. A loaf of bread rose on the counter. Not wanting to disturb her, Christi decided to feed the kitten herself. She placed the cat on the counter and opened a cupboard.

As she reached for a saucer, Marguerite's sharp voice stopped her. "What do you require?"

"Some milk for Fumée."

"She already eat."

"Oh, well..." Christi replaced the saucer in the cupboard and mouthed, "Sorry," to the kitten who still purred with expectation.

"I do not permit cats on my counter."

"Sorry." Christi lifted Fumée off the counter and lowered her to the floor. The kitten twirled around her legs, meowing. Christi spotted the bowl of dried cat food next to the pantry and pointed Fumée in its direction. She crunched contentedly on kibbles, and Christi, every muscle aching as if she'd gone fifteen rounds with the heavyweight champion, slogged her way across the kitchen to visit Rosane next door.

"She was the favorite of everyone," Marguerite said, gaze still locked on the pages of her book.

"Pardon me?"

"She had everything. And me, nothing."

Christi lowered herself to the chair next to Marguerite. "I'm sorry, Marguerite, I have no idea what you're talking about."

"Caroline."

The lens-magnified eyes blazed with righteous fervor and something darker, more purulent. Her skin was almost green with the taint of her jealousy.

"My mother?" Christi said tentatively.

"She have everything. Everyone love Caroline." She thumped her fist on the table. The cold cup of coffee skipped in its saucer. Fumée jumped and arched like a Halloween cat. "But Philippe, he love me."

Christi had no idea what to say or where this discussion was leading.

"Now is my turn." Marguerite's hand clenched around the fragile cup with such force that it shattered. Coffee soaked through the pages of her book, but Marguerite didn't move.

Christi reached for the rag Marguerite kept beside the sink and mopped up the mess. She carefully extricated the broken pieces of china from Marguerite's hand. Red mixed with the muddy caramel of the coffee. Her stomach rolled at the sight, then settled.

"You're bleeding," Christi said, trying to rouse Marguerite from her stupor. She found a clean towel and twisted it around Marguerite's hand in an improvised bandage. "You have to have these cuts seen to, Marguerite."

But Marguerite wasn't listening. Only the husk of her body remained in the kitchen. The rest had shrunk inward to a world only she could see.

Christi tried to locate Armand, but could not find him anywhere. When she returned to the kitchen, Marguerite sat in the same position, still staring at something far away. Christi checked the bandage. The blood had stopped flowing. Marguerite would be all right.

The fire inside Christi's stomach picked up intensity. Head swimming, she reached into her pocket for the medicine the doctor had given her and downed a tablet. "I'm going next door," she told Marguerite. She had to get away from this nightmare of a house, if only long enough to find her feet. "I'll be back soon."

Marguerite gave no sign she'd heard a word.

"MADEMOISELLE LAWRENCE, I did not expect to see you today." Francine Beaulieu opened the door wide to admit Christi. Francine wore jeans and a colorful sweater with swirls of rose, royal blue and ivory. She was wiping black ink from her fingers with a tissue. "Monsieur Moreau said you would be in the hospital for another day."

"I was discharged this morning. Is Rosane here?"

"No, I am sorry. She went to school with Isabelle. They should return soon. Please come in." Francine led her toward the back of the house and into a kitchen that was sunny in spite of the gloom outside.

"I don't want to interrupt your day."

"*Pas du tout!* I have to take a break anyway. My printer will not cooperate today. Let me make you a cup of tea."

"Thank you." Christi sat at the table while Francine fussed with a kettle in the shape and color of an apple. Air redolent with cinnamon filled the room. "What do you do?"

"I write a cooking column for the local newspaper." Francine's bright blue eyes twinkled with pride. "Today I am trying a new recipe. Now that you are here, you can be, how do you say?…my guinea pig."

"With pleasure." Christi worried the corner of the red, green and yellow woven placemat. Hopefully the medicine would allow her stomach to remain a sleeping volcano. "I hope Rosane has been behaving."

"Oh, she is fine. Do not worry. Isabelle is glad to have a friend. There are not many children in this neighborhood." Francine plucked two green glass dessert plates from a cupboard, then reached into a drawer for a spatula. She sat at the table and proceeded to cut two large squares from the coffeecake cooling on a trivet. "This house has been in my family for many generations. It is too hard to leave so much history.''

Christi hoped the history housed in this home was happier than the one hiding behind the stones of Armand's house. ''I can understand the tie of roots.''

Francine poured hot water over tea, then set a cup before Christi. ''Leave a few sips of tea at the bottom and I will read you your fortune.''

''My fortune?'' Christi chuckled and wrapped her hands around the warmth of the cup.

''I am known for my ability to read tea leaves. It is a hobby.'' Francine tucked a strand of shoulder-length hair behind her ear. A pair of blue budgies chirped in their corner cage. ''How did you meet Monsieur Moreau?'' Curiosity skated in Francine's eyes. ''He is Rosane's father, *non?*''

Christi made a show of tasting the coffeecake. Slivered almonds studded the cinnamon crumb topping. Currants dotted the cake. ''This is very good.''

''Thank you. I am experimenting with flours. This time I used a soy mixture.'' She forked a piece into her mouth and nodded. ''I am sorry. I did not mean to pry.''

''It's all right. I'm just not sure where to start.'' Daniel had a way of twisting her all up inside. ''I met him while he was studying music, and he left before I knew I was pregnant. I didn't know I'd find him again when I came here.''

''How happy for you! Let me see your cup.'' Francine swirled the contents of Christi's cup, then turned the cup upside down in the saucer. When what remained of the tea had drained out, she turned the cup right side up again and peered inside.

A smile budded, then bloomed on her face. "Ah, I see love. I see a voyage." She frowned. "Oh, and danger. Great danger. You must take care."

"I will." Christi touched Francine's hand. "Thank you for watching over Rosane. Knowing she's safe here with you is a great relief."

"I am glad to keep her."

Christi picked at the almonds with her fork. "It's only for one more night."

"It is not a problem."

Christi put her fork down and pushed her plate away. How could she transmit her fear, yet not invite a host of questions she'd rather not answer. "It's very important that Rosane not go to the Langeliers' home. Monsieur Langelier isn't well."

"I will tuck her in myself." Francine covered Christi's hand with her own reassuring one. "Do not worry."

"Thank you. It means a lot to me."

"I am a mother, too. I understand." Francine lifted the teapot. "Would you like more tea?"

"I don't know how I can repay you for imposing on you so much. You barely know us and you've been so kind."

Francine's face creased with the mischievous smile of a pixie. "How about an invitation to the wedding?"

"What wedding?"

"Yours and Daniel Moreau's." Francine chuckled. "The tea leaves are rarely wrong."

Christi shook her head and her cheeks burned from the flashfire of her blush. "I don't think—"

She was saved from further embarrassment when the front door burst open and in spilled two giggling girls. They tracked in muddy slush, and Francine shooed them back to the foyer before they reached the kitchen.

"How was your day?" Christi heard Francine ask the girls as they shucked coats and boots.

"Great!" Rosane stuffed her mittens in her coat pockets. "You should've seen Isabelle. She put that nasty Marc Marchand in his place."

Hands on hips, Francine glowered at the girls. "You girls didn't get into a fight, did you?"

"He started it." Isabelle kicked her boots under the hall bench. "He pushed Rosane into the fence at recess and called her nasty names. He was going to beat her up. So I decked him. He ran away calling for his mother."

The girls wrapped their arms around each other and giggled as they mocked the poor boy. *"Maman! Maman!"*

"Isabelle!" Francine chided.

Isabelle shrugged and scampered up. "Well, no one's going to mess with us now."

"There are other ways. We'll talk about it later." Francine twirled Rosane toward the kitchen. "Rosane, you have a visitor."

"Who?"

"Your mother."

Instantly, the smile slid from Rosane's face. Christi rose on shaky legs to hug her. Rosane pulled away and went to sit at the table next to Isabelle.

"Would you like some milk with your cookies?" Francine asked.

"S'il vous plaît," Rosane said.

Isabelle dug into the cookie jar and pulled out a

handful of molasses cookies and shared her boon with Rosane. *"Moi, aussi."*

"Sounds like you had an interesting day at school," Christi ventured.

Rosane reached under the table for Isabelle's hand. "I don't have to go, do I?"

"No, you can stay with Isabelle for a while longer."

Francine requested Isabelle's help in another room, leaving mother and daughter to face each other across the table.

Rosane kicked the chair's leg in an annoying rhythm and dunked half a cookie into her glass of milk. "Daniel came to see me last night."

A shot of ice catapulted through Christi's veins. She hid her shiver with a sip of tea. "What did you talk about?"

Rosane shrugged as if she didn't care. "He said you were in the hospital because your stomach was hurting and that you'd be fine after you rested for a bit."

"He's right. I'm going to be just fine."

Like a scientist performing an experiment of worldly consequence, Rosane dipped a cookie half into her milk and observed the submerged end through the side of the glass. "Is he really my father?"

"Yes."

Rosane lifted the soaked cookie and watched the milk-laden section plop onto a plate. "Why didn't he want me?"

Christi wanted to pull her daughter into her lap and wrap her arms around her. But another rejection would cut too deep right now, so she twined her fingers under the table. "He didn't know about you, honey. And then he thought I might not like it if he came back."

"Would you?"

Rosane was so still, her eyes so big that the pressure of giving her the right answer drove a nail right through her gut, setting off ripples of unease. "I'm not sure how I feel at the moment."

The annoying tempo of sock-muted kicks on chair legs resumed. "He gave me a letter."

"What did it say?"

"I haven't read it yet." Another careless shrug that hid the fear of another disappointment. She hadn't saved Rosane from anything after all.

Whatever else was between her and Daniel, he did care for his daughter. She'd heard his heart in *Berceuse pour un Ange*—the song he'd written for his baby daughter. "Read it. He loves you."

"Okay." Rosane twirled the end of her ponytail around a finger. "Armand said that you wanted to marry Daniel and that Daniel would send me away like his father did with his kids."

To tell a child she wasn't wanted and compound the cruelty by telling her her own father would send her away from the people she loved was plain evil. "Armand lied to you. Daniel wanted us both to live with him and be a family."

"Are you going to marry him?"

Christi hesitated, then settled on, "I don't know."

"Mom, you wouldn't leave me, would you?"

"Oh, never, honey. I could never leave you. You are the love of my life." Muscles quivering, she drew her daughter into her lap and kissed the top of her head.

"I missed you." Rosane snuggled closer.

"I missed you, too." Christi gently stroked Rosane's hair. "Listen, there's something else we have to talk about. Tonight, Daniel is playing at a concert, and he asked me to go listen to his music. You'll spend the night with Isabelle. Okay?"

"Okay."

"I don't want you going over to Armand's house, is that understood?"

"Sure." Rosane relaxed against Christi's shoulder. "Will you come kiss me good-night when the concert is over?"

For the first time in days, she thought things would work out. "I wouldn't miss it for the world."

THE THEATER WORLD had an old belief that if the rehearsal was a mess, the performance was bound to be a smash. If there was any truth to the old saw, Daniel knew tonight's concert would be a raging success.

Daniel paced the length of the art gallery used for private receptions. He saw none of the paintings, but the room was quiet and he needed to get away from the chaos that surrounded the theater.

After worrying about Christiane and Rosane all last night, he hadn't slept a wink. He didn't in the least feel inspired to perform in public tonight.

He should've realized the day wasn't going to be a smooth one when he found his two back tires slashed first thing this morning. Armand had probably sent his henchman, Célestin Cadieu, to do the job. Christiane had not answered her hospital room phone. The taxi he'd called got him to the hospital too late. And when he'd reached the house, she was in the shower. He'd wanted to stay, but obligations tugged him in opposite directions. Given Christiane's cold shoulder, he'd opted to go to the theater and make sure Armand had not set up a trap there. Now she was back in that house of horrors and no one was answering the phone.

Things had not gotten better once he'd arrived at the theater. The piano was off-key. The fiddler couldn't find his bow. The background scenery fell and almost crushed a stagehand. The whole world seemed to have tilted on its axis and there was nothing he could do.

"Daniel, there you are." His manager, Jean-Paul, trotted toward him. "The reporters are waiting for you in the foyer."

"You handle them."

"No can do." Jean-Paul bounced around Daniel like the overeager bulldog he was. "After that mess with the photographer on Saturday, you have to be the one to charm the leeches. They won't believe anything coming from me."

"Jean-Paul—"

"Da-niel. It's your image that's at stake. Don't you care?"

"Actually, no." Daniel gestured at the silk tie hanging loose at his neck. "Help me with this."

Jean-Paul reached for the tie at Daniel's neck. "I told you it was a mistake to get mixed up with that girl."

"No, the mistake was putting it off for so long." Daniel massaged the painful thumping at his temples. "Have you seen Armand yet?"

"I have better things to do than chase a cranky old man around."

"He's dangerous." Daniel snapped away from Jean-Paul's iron hand at his throat. "Ow, that's too tight."

"How do you expect me to knot it properly if you keep moving?"

Daniel shoved his hands into his pockets and forced himself to stand still. "Did you send a car for Christiane?"

"Yes. And I promised the driver a handsome fee to see her safely inside the theater. There you go." Jean-Paul stepped back to admire his handiwork.

"I want you to stay by her side every minute of my performance."

Jean-Paul's eyes rolled back and he shook his head. "No can do. I'll see her seated, but then I've got other fish to fry. Nothing's going to happen, okay?" He headed toward the door. "Get your act together quick."

But Daniel couldn't shake the sense of wrongness, of desperation that clung to him like a second skin. He had to know Christiane was safe. "Jean-Paul—"

"Da-niel." A wry grin creased his bulldog jowls. "What could possibly happen in a crowded theater?"

Too much. What if she left her seat? What if he lost her in the crowd? What if he couldn't get to her when she needed him?

"Daniel?" Jean-Paul's bark cut into his gloomy thoughts. "The reporters."

Daniel grunted. "Give me a minute."

"Don't keep them waiting too long." Jean-Paul strode out the door, and Daniel had no doubt that his manager would keep the reporters at bay until Daniel could compose himself into the charming public persona Jean-Paul had so carefully schooled.

Slowly Daniel made his way to the foyer. Everybody wanted something from him. And all he wanted was to disappear to that imaginary house in the woods with his music, his daughter and Christiane. He raked a hand through his hair and took in a deep breath before he opened the heavy door. As promised, a dozen hungry leeches rushed to suck away more of his life.

ARMAND INSPECTED his appearance in the full-length mirror on the inside of the armoire door. He tugged on his vest, fiddled with the knot of his tie and brushed away a nonexistent piece of lint from the sleeve of his tuxedo jacket. With a satisfied nod, he turned away from the mirror and closed the armoire door.

"This is the day, Caro." He lifted his arms and turned. "What do you think?"

He propped a bony hip on the corner of the desk and looked down at Caroline. "You don't approve of my plans, do you? It doesn't matter. I don't need your approval, *chère cousine*. My glory arrives tonight."

From the file cabinet, he extracted the jeweler's box he'd saved for so many years. Rose's locket—the devil's gift to his bride. Not just part of the legend, but reality. He'd paid a dear price for this precious antique. The Master will be pleased.

He opened the box and fingered the fine gold chain, then pressed the button on the side of the locket. The top sprang open. "Too bad I can't wait for Rosane to grow up. Her virgin youth would give me mine back. Think how much more I could accomplish with a young body. How many more families I could create."

Sighing, he closed the locket with a snap and carefully laid it in its velvet box. He slipped the case in his left pocket. He patted his breast pocket and touched the outline of the ceremonial knife. Then he checked his right pocket and felt the weight of the small round box it held.

"I have everything I need."

He grabbed his coat off the bed. "Rejoice, Caro. You will soon see your daughter again."

Chapter Thirteen

The hall lights dimmed and the overhead bank of lights brought the stage to life. Daniel took a deep breath and stepped onto the illuminated floorboards. Applause echoed through the hall.

Jean-Paul hadn't exaggerated; the house was full tonight. Caterpillars crawled around his stomach. Never had this happened before. Performing always came easily. Shutting off the crowd and focusing on his music was second nature. So why did tonight, of all nights, have to be his first encounter with stage fright?

He flexed his fingers, trying to bring some warmth back to them and made his way across the stage. The piano's new placement momentarily took him aback. It was more to the left than during rehearsal, and he had to check his long strides to stop in time. As he bowed to his audience, he searched the front row for Christiane.

When he spotted her, some of the caterpillars calmed. The red of her dress made her look bloodless and the white shawl emphasized the boniness of her shoulders. She should be home in bed, not here. But she was safe in her seat. And for now that was all that mattered. When this blasted concert was over, he'd make sure she rested and healed. Jean-Paul was right. What could possibly happen in a crowded theater?

With great show, he took his place at the piano bench. Hands poised over the keys, he willed his mind to concentrate. *Fugue de Pègasse* would get things started with a bang and relieve some of his pent-up frustration.

When he played the first note, the rest of the caterpillars stilled. The audience disappeared. He was one with the music, and he performed every bar with all his heart…for Christiane.

ROSANE TURNED in the twin bed that matched Isabelle's and looked out the window to the clouds, soft and gray against the black sky. A fat one drifted by the open curtains. It looked like an overloaded water balloon ready to burst. She and Isabelle had gushed over the red sequined bodice and the flowing, gauzy layers of the skirt of Mom's dress. Red fire and ice. Mom had looked like a fairy princess.

What would it be like to wear a pretty dress like Mom's? To listen to a concert in a fancy theater? When would she be old enough to go, too? She remembered the tiny sandwiches and pastries Mom had once brought back from a charity ball she'd attended. Magic, pure magic.

She peered at Isabelle's lime-green alarm clock and saw it was almost eleven. Flipping to her back, she laced her fingers behind her head.

She thought of Daniel then, of how handsome he'd looked in the tuxedo he wore during the television interview on the news. Mom had said she should read his letter. But she hadn't wanted to read it in front of Isabelle just in case she didn't like what was in it. He wasn't the prince of her mother's stories, that was for sure. She didn't want to like Daniel, but she wanted to know that he had cared for her.

She reached for the backpack beside the bed. Careful not to make any noise, she opened the padded envelope. But the light was too low to read, so she tiptoed to the window seat and cocked the paper toward the streetlamp below.

"21 November," the letter read.

My Dearest Angel,
    Today you are one year old. I'm not very good with words, but I want to let you know that, even though I can't be with you, you will always hold a part of my heart. This lullaby is my gift to you.
Your father.

Rosane refolded the stiff creases. She fingered the tape through the padded envelope. A song just for her. She spied a cassette player on the toy shelf. A tape fell as she tried to extract the player from the messy shelf, clattering on the wood floor. She quickly glanced in Isabelle's direction, relieved to find Isabelle still sleeping.

At the window seat, she tucked her feet beneath her and inserted Daniel's tape into the player. She adjusted the headphones and pressed the play button.

"This is for you, my darling daughter," Daniel's voice rang through her head. "A lullaby for an angel."

The music started slow and soft. Rosane drew up her legs and hugged them. She closed her eyes and rested her forehead on her knees. The music built note by note, like stitches on a blanket, and surrounded her with warmth. The last note fell like a kiss on a sleeping baby's forehead. The player droned as the batteries powered the tape to its end, then clicked off.

She wiped tears from her eyes and hugged her knees tighter. But the tears wouldn't go away. She grabbed the doll Marguerite had given her and pressed it to her chest. But it was cold and prickly, and she needed someone warm. She couldn't wait until Mom got back from the concert. She needed a hug now. Sniffing, she grabbed a sweater and pulled it over her pajama top. *Fumée.*

Placing her feet just so to avoid the creak of tattletale floorboards, she held on to Amélie's stiff hand and made her way down the stairs. In the living room, the television still played. She paused and took a quick peek. Isabelle's father snored in front of the hockey game on the television. Isabelle's mother was nowhere in sight, but the soft tapping of computer keys clickety-clacked from the small office down the hall.

Holding her breath, Rosane sneaked past the living room entrance. In the foyer, she stuffed her feet in boots and reached for her coat. As the front door's hinges complained, Rosane heard Isabelle's father call, "Francine?"

Rosane quickly shut the door behind her and hid in the evergreen bush beside the front steps. Heavy snowflakes melted as they landed in her hair. She waited, crouched, but no one came to the door, so she ran, slipping and sliding on the fresh snow bursting from the sky, to the back door of Armand's house.

The handle turned easily. Breath held, she listened.

A hush hung over the house, like it was holding a secret. Then the slow tick-tock of the clock in the foyer rolled into the kitchen. As she closed the door, she smiled at the familiar sound of crunching kibbles. "Fumée!"

She jogged into the darkened kitchen. "There you are you silly kitten. Eating again. You're going to be so fat, I won't be able to carry you home." Giggling, she dropped the doll and picked up the purring kitten. "Want to go on a sleepover?"

She pressed the cat to her chest and zipped the coat over the squirming animal. "It's cold out there." She patted the lump of cat. "You'll stay warm in there."

Fumée pushed her head out the neck opening and rewarded Rosane with a sandpaper kiss. Rosane was heading toward the door when the sound of crying from the back room where Marguerite did her sewing floated down the hall like a song out of tune.

With only the light of a candle, Marguerite rocked in the rocking chair, clutching a folder—the kind Mom always took home from work—to her chest. A stream of tears ran from her face and splotched on the file.

"Marguerite, are you all right?" Rosane tentatively entered the room, spooked by the sharp shadows dancing on Marguerite's face. Why was she sitting in the dark like that, crying?

Marguerite glanced up and a smile bounced her lips up, making her look like a scary clown. "There you are, *petite*." Using the tail of her apron, she lifted her glasses and wiped the tears. "I have missed you so much."

Rosane drew closer to the rocking chair. "I'm only next door at Isabelle's."

Marguerite looked confused. Rosane's heart thumped in her chest and a small voice inside her belly screamed at her to run. She started to back up, suddenly afraid to let Marguerite out of her sight.

"Non, petite. Viens ici." She hefted her bulk out of the chair and opened her arms. *"Grand-maman* will take care of you."

Rosane tripped over a footstool and fell on her back. Her breath whooshed out of her lungs. Fumée's claws dug into her neck and a warm trickle of blood glided down her skin. Fumée meowed in distress. Rosane patted the cat braced to her chest. "Shh."

The hall clock chimed once—a long, slow bong that sounded like an earthquake. Marguerite paused. Her nose twitched as if she smelled danger. Her eyes darted about as if some sort of monster hid in the shadows of the room. Then like the anteater's tongue she'd seen at the zoo, Marguerite's arms whipped out. Marguerite grabbed her and yanked her to her feet. *"Viens, petite,* we do not have much time."

AT THE SOUND of the warning chime after intermission, Christi took her seat. Daniel's manager had dogged her every step and seen her back inside the hall. Her search for Armand in the crowd had proved fruitless. If not here, now, then where and when? A leaden weariness weighed her limbs as if she were one big beanbag. Her head gave every indication that cotton candy filled it. And her stomach ached with the lump of wax that seemed lodged there. She wanted a warm bed, a fluffy pillow and days and days of mindless, reenergizing sleep.

She glanced at the stage and saw Daniel peeking from the wings. Their gazes locked and an ounce of worry appeared to melt from his face. She wasn't going to think about Daniel right now. She had enough on her mind with Armand and the obsession he planned to fulfill tonight. She'd worn a mental shield against the effects of Daniel's music, closed her eyes against the mesmerizing effect of his hands, and still the first half of the program had seemed to last forever.

The lights were dimming when one of the ushers whispered to her, *"Vous avez un appel, mademoiselle."*

"A call? Who?" Rosane? No, she was safe.

"Francine Beaulieu."

Francine? Christi's heart hammered against her chest, acid spilled against the already raw walls of her stomach and panic trooped up her spine. Francine wouldn't call unless it was urgent. Rosane. Oh, no, something had happened to Rosane. Was that why she wasn't able to find Armand? Because he was over at the Beaulieu's home?

She stumbled out of her seat. The usher caught her elbow and steadied her. "This way, *mademoiselle*." He clicked on his beam to light their way.

To the sound of applause, Christi followed the usher to the manager's office. He opened the door, let her in and closed the door softly behind her. Only a banker's light burned on the desk, making the room feel as if it had no corners. The phone was off the hook. Christi hurried toward it. "Francine?"

The phone was dead.

From behind her, the lock's mechanism tumbled. She whirled to find Armand leaning against the door. Her shawl slid to the floor.

"Have a seat, *ma chère*. It is not quite time for our performance yet."

Pulse pounding, stomach acid spiking, she forced herself to lean nonchalantly against the desk. He was a weak old man. Any other day, she could've taken him without batting an eye. But her recent hospital stay had drained her strength. She'd burned precious energy worrying about Rosane as she'd rushed to answer her call for help. To escape, she'd have to hoard what little energy she had left and use it precisely. A paperweight caught her attention. She shifted her weight and inched her way toward it. "What do you want from me?"

"Everything." He showed his palms like a magician offering proof he had nothing up his sleeves.

She stretched her fingers to touch the cold stone behind her. The paperweight slipped from her sweaty grasp. "You've been dancing around the issue, hinting, since I got here, but I still don't know what you want from me."

Armand reached into his suit jacket and brought out a pack of cigarettes. He lit one and took a long drag. "You are familiar with the legend of Rose Latulippe."

Christi nodded as she brought her hand back to her side and wiped her sweat-slicked palms on her dress. "I don't see how it has anything to do with me."

"The Master fell in love with the beautiful Rose. He wanted her for his bride. Unfortunately, he was foiled at the last minute and lost Rose."

"So?"

"You are a descendant of Rose."

"And?" This time her fingers clung to the stone paperweight.

"The Master still needs a bride."

"Your master doesn't exist. How do you propose to give me to him?"

"I will offer him your soul, and in return, he will grant me my wish."

"Which is?" Keep him talking. Keep him distracted. She shifted her weight for a better grip.

"Eternal life, of course." Armand puffed on his cigarette. Smoke swirled in front of his face as if he were already part of the underworld.

"That'll never work." She steeled herself. She would only get one shot. "Even if you manage to kill me, you'll be arrested and spend the rest of your *eternal* life in jail."

"You are too young to understand the mysteries of life. There are powers at work here that only a few can harness." He spoke in the low tones of a superior to a lesser. Ashes from the tip of his cigarette dropped to the carpet.

"And you can?"

His smile was radiant with rapture.

She almost felt sorry for him. An obsessed young man had erased the boundary between reality and fantasy, until the fantasy was so real, he had to have it at all cost. He'd wasted his life searching for something that didn't exist, something he could never have. "And exactly how do you plan to achieve this exchange?"

"I have prepared the most wonderful ceremony. It will cast a spell over everyone." His head tipped back in laughter that bounced against the walls and shivered through her bones.

She balanced the paperweight in the palm of her hand. Just as she hurled the paperweight at Armand's head, he doubled over in a coughing fit. The paperweight missed him, dented the wall and crashed to the carpet. For a moment, they stared at each other. His eyes were dark stones of molten rage.

"That was a mistake, *ma chère*. Nothing will keep me from my destiny tonight."

"CHRISTIANE isn't in her seat." Jacket flapping like the black wings of a crow, Daniel paced offstage with the restlessness of a caged panther. "Where is she?"

Jean-Paul handed him a bottle of water. "I don't know. I walked her right to her row."

"Find her now. Make sure she's all right."

"She's probably in the ladies' room."

Daniel wrenched off the cap from the water bottle. "Go check."

"She's perfectly fine."

"I *need* to know." Daniel recapped the water bottle and started toward the stairs. "Never mind, I'll go look for her myself."

"You will do no such thing." Hands on hips, Jean-Paul pivoted to block Daniel's exit. "You have to appear on that stage in less than a minute. You can't disappoint your audience with a less than brilliant second half."

"Then go find her."

"I will." Jean-Paul pushed him toward a chair. "Now relax. You're not acting like yourself and that worries me."

Daniel sprang up, raked a hand through his hair and started pacing again. "I'll be fine as soon as I know Christiane is safe in her seat."

"All right, all right." Jean-Paul left mumbling

something about temperamental artists and regretting the day he got involved in the business.

"Showtime!" a stagehand shouted, and the curtains started to rise.

Daniel buttoned his jacket, straightened his tie and downed half the bottle of water. If he could catch a glimpse of Christiane safe in her seat before he had to perform, he could get through the second half of the show without losing his mind.

"HELP! Someone help me!" Christi shouted until her lungs burned.

With a surprising burst of strength, Armand shoved Christi hard against the wall. Her head rapped against the sharp edge of a massive wall sculpture. Stars streaked her vision. Her back slammed against some other protrusion. Air vanished from her lungs. Stunned, Christi slid down the wall. As if someone had pulled a shade, the world turned gray.

Armand took advantage of her immobility to wrap her shawl tightly around her wrists. While she still struggled to find her breath, he yanked her to a standing position and dragged her toward a chair. She gulped in mouthfuls of air, choked on them and gasped again for air.

He shoved her into the chair and bound her ankles with his tie, then pushed her forward and rubbed her back until her breath returned.

She gulped in air. *"Help!"*

"Shout all you want. No one will hear you. We are too far away from the fray.

"Let me go!"

"I cannot do that." Armand rounded the chair and faced her. His eyes seemed like glowing embers. "It really is not a good idea for you to get so excited. The doctor said you had to avoid stress.''

And being murdered wasn't stressful? *"Help!"*

"I have something for you." He reached into his pocket and extracted a velvet jeweler's box she recognized from her foray into his office. He opened the box and turned it so she could see the locket nestled on the satin backing. "The Master gave it to Rose. Now you shall wear it.''

He extracted a knife from the inside breast pocket of his jacket. A scream rolled inside her as the tip of the knife neared her throat. *"Help!"*

"Do not move. I do not want to cut you."

The knife slipped under the delicate chain that held a filigree cross that belonged to her mother. A puff of acrid smoke burst from the chain as the knife severed the links. She jerked back in the chair and the tip of the knife nicked the skin under her jaw. The silver cross skittered across the desk and the chain slid into the bodice of her dress.

Armand rounded the chair and secured the ruby encrusted locket around her neck. She dug her heels into the carpet and with all her might, propelled the chair backward, shoving Armand into the wall. The chair bounced off her prey and spun around, bringing her face-to-face with Armand. Adrenaline, his manic belief that he was moments from eternal life, gave him strength just as it sapped hers. His fingers snaked out and gripped her jaw like talons. The low growl of his voice reverberated through the hollow of her bones. "You cannot escape your fate."

"Help! Someone help—" A linen gag cut her off midscream. A fresh surge of panic skittered through her veins, bleeding the rest of her strength.

He stood and dusted the arms of his jacket. "It is time."

Staying out of reach of her feet, he sliced the tie at her ankles. Before she could swivel to kick him, he yanked her up. With one glacial hand around her waist and the other pressing the tip of the knife under the rib covering her heart, he urged her forward. With reverence, he whispered, "This will be the greatest moment of your life."

Chapter Fourteen

Two more pieces and this nightmare will be over. Daniel let the last note of *Fantômes et Fantaisies* linger in the air, then announced, "The last two pieces I will play tonight are new compositions. The first, *Trésor Retrouvé,* is for someone very special. The second, *Une Rose à Minuit,* is one commissioned by the Arts Committee especially for this Mardi Gras performance."

In the sea of black suits and bright dresses, he searched for Christiane's red dress. Hands poised over the keys, his heart flubbed once at the empty seat she should have occupied. Where was she?

The silence stretched and murmurs from the crowd reminded him that they were expecting him to play. His fingers found the keys, but he could only give them half his attention. Part of him searched for the tendrils of essence that were Christiane.

THE PRODDING TIP of Armand's knife dug into Christi's side. The linen gag stretched her mouth at an uncomfortable angle. Worst of all, they'd encountered no one in the dark backstage corridors.

Shouldn't there be people back here? Stagehands? Managers? Reporters?

She balked like a mule when he pressed her toward the catwalk access. The knife only dug deeper, sending a shower of red sequins like crystallized droplets of blood raining down to her feet.

After the first few stairs, she tried to kick out at Armand behind her. But he kept too close to her and her blows landed ineffectively. One of her red satin pumps fell off and clattered to the floor below just as the music started to fade. She promptly launched off her other shoe to attract attention. But the sound of the shoe hitting the floorboards was lost in the raucous applause of the crowd.

Her stockinged feet slipped on the cold metal stair. Armand's knife ripped into the bodice, sending another small shower of sequins to the floor below. Panic cranked up another notch. She needed to attract attention. But how? The crowd was entranced by Daniel's music. No one haunted the backstage area. *Think, Christi.* There had to be a way.

"It's you or your daughter," Armand rasped as he pressed her upward. "The choice is yours. Either way, I will not be cheated. I *will* get what I deserve."

She wanted to scream, but the gag was in the way. "What have you done to Rosane?" It came out a garble of grunts.

"I am holding her in a safe place. She will remain safe as long as you cooperate."

He was lying. Had to be. He'd faked the phone call. Rosane was safe in bed at Francine's.

"You think I do not tell the truth. But can you really take the chance that I am?"

No, she couldn't. Her chest squeezed tight. What

could she do? The same thing her mother had done. She had to stay alive. She had to rescue her daughter.

The narrow catwalk, high above the hall, stretched across the stage and offered easy access to the banks of lights. Armand prodded her forward. "On you go."

Her body followed. Her mind searched every dark recess for a way to foil Armand. Whatever happened here tonight, Rosane wasn't safe. The only way to help her was to stay alive.

A third of the way across the metal grid, an object that looked strangely like a birdcage blocked their way. Once he had her in there, how could she get out? She jerked to a stop, wrenching her torso back to unbalance Armand. If she could send him over the edge, he would die in the fall. He wavered, but didn't loosen his grip. She tried to bump him again, but this time he was ready.

"You or your daughter. If I do not reach my glory tonight, she *will* die." He shoved Christi unceremoniously into the cage. She hit a rounded bar, bruising her shoulder, and crumpled to the bottom. He entered the cage and closed the door behind him. From his pocket, he extracted a small round box.

As she struggled to stand, he reached down and held her bound wrists in a viselike grip. With a small black feather, her rubbed a yellowish salve into her palms. A sharp pain burned into her skin and sent numbing prickles, like invading fleas, racing through her body. Terror filled every cell, poured from her sweat, swelled her tongue until she could taste nothing but its sharp tang.

"With the magic," Armand said, his voice a blanket of compassion, as he slipped the box and feather into his pocket, "there will be no pain."

After a few moments, he cut the knotted shawl from her wrists. He removed the gag and smoothed the corners of her mouth stretched tight by the linen.

She could've been a rag doll for all the control she had over her limbs. She could not feel her feet, her hands, not even the riot surely producing chaos in her stomach. Only her brain wasn't frozen into place. A scream spasmed in her chest, clawed its way up her throat and eked out in a stressed mewl that barely reached her own ears. She was both heavier than cast bronze and lighter than a ghost. Disembodied. Not real. The edges of her vision were growing black. *Oh, please, no. Don't let me go blind.*

She was beyond panic, beyond hysteria. Then, just as she thought she was going to fold into herself and disappear into the black, a surprising sense of calm filled her.

If she gave in to fear, she would die. To save Rosane, she had to stay alive. Survival instinct kicked in.

Armand returned the knife to his pocket, then lifted her and propped her against the side of the cage. Tired after his exertion, he wiped his brow with the sleeve of his free arm. He checked his watch. As Daniel announced his two last pieces, a manic glow burned in Armand's eyes. He slicked the sides of his greased hair and smoothed his jacket. His left hand held her propped against the side of the cage. His right hand held the black-handled knife at her heart. Then he stood, legs slightly apart, and nodded once.

The music started. The notes floated up to her,

wrung tears from her heart. Her song. Daniel was playing her song.

With an ominous creak, the cage started to descend, rotating slowly on its axis. Below them, she recognized Célestin Cadieu, hidden from the audience by the stage curtain, operating the mechanism that controlled the cage's descent.

As they passed the lights, their heat burned her face, but registered nowhere else. She closed her eyes against their brightness, offered up a desperate prayer.

When she opened them again, everything came to her in sharp detail. The black piano. The ripples of music moving across her brain like a caress. Daniel's body bent over his instrument, his beautiful hands a blur. The rounded edges of the stage. The balconies with their gold trim and burgundy accents, flanked by columns painted an antique rose. The fiddler furiously rasping at his instrument. The enthralled audience. The smell of sweat. Her own? Armand's spicy aftershave. The gleaming blade of knife at her breast.

Time hung and played itself in slow motion, one frame at a time.

She cried for everything she would lose and found that in her tears there was power. The only way to break Armand's hold on her was to fight evil with the only thing it feared—love. "Daniel…"

DANIEL… His name whispered across his brain, like faraway reeds. The insistent silvery shrill tugged his head up. There, suspended in a golden cage, was Christiane, and Armand held a knife poised at her breast. The sight was a syringe straight into his heart. His blood went cold. Fear like poison rushed through his veins. His fingers turned to stiff sticks, but kept playing as if they instinctively knew that if they stopped, he would lose his chance to save Christiane. Play to Armand's expectations. He ended *Trésor Retrouvé* and launched right into *Une Rose à Minuit,* just as Armand had heard him rehearse.

"Jean-Paul!" he rasped through clenched teeth so the audience would stay entranced.

"Daniel?" Jean-Paul's voice yipped from the wings. "What's wrong?"

Daniel jerked his head toward the cage above him, using his music as a cover. "Call security. Now. He's going to kill her."

The only way to save Christiane was to keep playing to cover the noise of the arriving security force. Never letting his gaze stray from hers, Daniel unleashed the feelings caged in his soul and told her with music what he could not say with words. *I love you. Hold on. I will find a way to save you.* He played as he'd never played—with all his heart and soul. He held nothing back.

"DO NOT LOOK so frightened," Armand said. Mania burned in his eyes, a fever so bright, nothing but death could stop it. "It will not hurt." He closed his eyes, seemed to feel the music below. "It is perfect. Can you feel the magic? I knew Daniel would come through and do it right. I was the first to recognize his talent."

Never had Daniel played so beautifully. Then as she lost herself in the notes, she thought she heard caution. *Get ready, get ready,* the melody seemed to say.

Flowing with the tempo building like heat, like

smoke, like the very edge of hell, Armand brought his arm back, ready to strike.

Get ready. She could hear her heart pounding, but couldn't feel its drum. A dead weight settled over her windpipe, rasping her breath. How much control did she have over the lead of her body?

A strident chord unraveled from the keyboard like a snowball racing downhill. Armand was startled, diverting the blade's arc. It struck the steel beside her arm, sparked. The crowd whispered its confusion. Voices like prongs of pitchforks spiked up through the air.

Daniel jumped onto the piano and launched himself at the cage. He caught the edge, setting the cage in frenzied motion.

With the movement came a plan. As if in a dream that seemed at once too real and too hazy, she waited. When the cage reached the top of its arc, Christi used the momentum to throw her drug-heavy body into Armand and knocked him off balance.

A look of disbelief crossed Armand's face, then everything speeded up. Their entwined bodies crashed against the door. With the ripping sound of steel giving way, the cage door pitched open. On stage, the fiddle screeched on.

"I will not be cheated!" Bellowing a curse worthy of a minion from Hades, Armand tumbled backward out of the cage, his clamped grip wrenching her out with him. They hurled through the air, everything around them a blur of colors and chaos, and landed in a mangled heap in the middle of the stage.

Chapter Fifteen

When Christi opened her eyes, Armand lay a few feet from her. His body had cushioned her fall. The jolt of the landing had rolled her off him. His limbs sprawled crookedly. His head was turned to one side with the flexibility only someone half his age could possible achieve. The blade of his knife was imbedded to the hilt in his chest. His eyes fluttered open, no longer aglow with his obsessive mania, but dull and flat as a corpse's. He coughed and sputtered blood all over his starched white shirt. As he looked past her shoulder, his hand rose feebly.

"Caro, wait for me!" His eyes closed. His head rolled to the left. And his hand dropped back to his side as if it no longer had a skeleton of bones to hold it up.

Armand's cry to his dead cousin lifted the audience from its spell. As one, they roared to their feet and scuttled like an ant pile disturbed by a child's stick. Utter confusion reigned. The deafening noise of their panic reverberated against the perfect acoustics of the hall, echoing like a chamber of horrors.

A bank of policemen scrambled to restore order.

Another struggled to push their way through the crowd, but made no headway.

"Christiane." Daniel lifted her to his chest. Through the tingle of returning feeling, she sensed the bracing support of his arms and sank into it. He hugged her so tight she thought she would suffocate and her last breath would be of the woodsy scent of his aftershave. "Are you all right?"

"I'm okay." She choked out the words past the grit coating her throat. "I'm alive. Rosane. I have to find her. Armand said—" She gulped much needed lubrication into her irritated throat. "He said he was holding her. He said if I didn't die, she would."

"She's safe at Francine's. I checked on her during intermission. Francine had just finished tucking them in."

Forcing her thick throat to move, she said, "Take me there. Please. I need to see Rosane."

"You need to go to the hospital."

"No. Rosane." Now that her body was tingling back to life, a mind-numbing weariness enveloped her. She wrapped a weak arm around Daniel's neck and buried her face in his chest. "Please, Daniel, hurry."

As Daniel started toward the exit, a policeman stopped him. "You can't leave. We have questions."

"They can wait. She needs medical attention." Spotting his manager across the stage, Daniel yelled, "Jean-Paul!"

Jean-Paul planted himself between the officer and Daniel. "I'll handle it. Go."

Like a single-minded bull, Daniel wound his way through corridors and pounded out into the parking area to his car. Somewhere between brusque urgency and tender care, he strapped her in the front seat of his Porsche. He sped away from the theater, and she was never so glad to see a building fade in the side mirror. The falling snow made the unplowed roads slushy. Even new tires could not keep the car from fishtailing now and then, forcing a growl from Daniel as he slowed.

"What did he do to you?" Daniel asked at a red light. Fat flakes of snow splotched in Rorschach patterns against the windshield. Their violent shapes had her imagining the worst possible outcome. The wipers scrubbed across the glass like frantic traffic cops trying to direct the blizzard. *Hurry, hurry, hurry,* the whining motor of the blades seemed to say.

She licked her dry lips. "Some sort of drug. On my hands. Paralyzed me. Hurry."

"Drugs? I'm taking you to the hospital."

"No! Daniel, please, I *have* to see Rosane."

"He drugged you, Christiane. You have no idea what he used. You need medical attention."

"No, see. I'm fine." She waved her hands and stamped her feet. "It's wearing off. I'm fine. Please, I need to see Rosane."

Daniel squeezed one of her hands, and she found some solace in the fact she could feel his flesh press against hers. "Armand is dead. Rosane is at Francine's. She's fine. You need—"

"I need to see her. I promised to tuck her in after the concert. I'm scared, Daniel. Armand—"

"She's safe." He fumbled for something in his pocket and brought out a cell phone. "I'll call and check on her, if that'll make you feel better."

"I have to see—"

"It's ringing." When the light turned green and the

driver in front of him didn't immediately move, Daniel leaned on his horn. "If Francine wakes Rosane and you talk to her, will you go to the hospital?"

"Yes." She'd promise anything to make sure her daughter was safe in her bed, that this was just some horrible nightmare that had finally come to an end.

But the drug Armand had spread like butter on her palms still itched its way through her veins. As much as it numbed her body, it seemed to heighten her mind, and she could not let go of the feeling that a dark thread of evil had wrapped itself around her precious daughter.

"MONSIEUR MOREAU?" Francine said, her voice filled with surprise.

"I need to talk to Rosane. Something happened at the theater tonight, and her mother wants to be sure she's safe in bed."

"Is Christiane all right?"

"She will be as soon as she knows Rosane is safe."

"I will go check on her."

Daniel covered the speaker with his thumb and said, "She's going up to check."

Francine had taken the phone with her. The stairs creaked as she made her way up to the second floor. The bedroom door seemed to whisper a secret as she pushed it open. At her gasp, Daniel swallowed the geyser of panic and forced himself to remain calm. "Francine? Is everything okay?"

"She is not here!" Francine's words sounded as distant as fog.

"Where is she?" Daniel demanded, keeping his eye on the road as he executed an illegal U-turn.

"I—I don't know," Francine stammered. "The girls went to bed hours ago. I tucked them in myself."

"When did you last see her?"

"I checked on them right before the news at eleven. They were both sleeping."

"Call the police." Daniel floored the accelerator.

"She's not there." Christiane's gaze scampered across his face. Her hand covered her trembling mouth. "Where is she?"

Daniel grabbed Christiane and trapped her against his side. "We're going to find her."

"Armand—"

"Is dead. He was at the theater and couldn't have touched her."

"He said he was holding her."

"We'll find her. I promise." Daniel rubbed his hand up and down her arm and drove toward Francine's home as fast as he could in the driving snow. They would find Rosane unharmed. He would do this one last thing before he set them free from the curse his father's sins had forced on them.

ONLY THE SLOW ticking of the grandfather clock in the entry hall greeted Daniel and Christiane as they entered Armand's house through the kitchen. The first thing they saw was the discarded doll lying akimbo on the floor.

Christiane picked it up and the look in her eyes was of pure terror.

"Wait here."

But Christiane didn't listen. She dogged his every footstep. Daniel flipped on lights as he checked each room on the first floor and called to Rosane. Her tiny footsteps, nearly covered by the falling snow, had pointed the way to Armand's house. The footsteps had stopped on the threshold of the back door. One set going in. None going out. She had to be in the house. The clock bonged once, deep and rolling like the growl of a *loup-garou,* a werewolf, with prey in sight.

When he rounded the curve of the stairs, he tripped over an old leather suitcase perched on a step. "Yours?"

Face whiter than the snow falling outside, Christiane shook her head.

Daniel resumed his climb, one careful step at a time. He knew the personality of each step, avoided the chatty ones, so he could hear any scrap of noise that would tell him where to find his daughter. "Rosane?"

He checked all the bedrooms, Armand's office, Marguerite's suite, and found them empty.

At the base of the stairs, Christiane was bent over the suitcase, examining its contents. "It's filled with Marguerite's clothes." She lifted a brand-new dress, basting thread still dangling from the collar. Her eyes grew impossibly wide. The black of her pupils sucked in the gray of her irises. "It's Rosane's size. Do you think Armand promised Marguerite Rosane?"

Before Daniel could answer, a loud thump, followed by the angry screech of a cat came from above. They both stared at the ceiling.

"Stay here." Daniel's haste ate up the stairs. He jumped at a brass handle on the off-white ceiling and pulled down a set of narrow stairs leading to the attic.

The sound of his heart pumping blood filled his ears as he climbed the stairs. He forced his heartbeat to slow and peered through the stuffy darkness above him. He'd played in this attic a thousand times as a child. There was nothing here except old trunks filled with moth-eaten clothes and forgotten memories. He reached for the chain to the attic light and pulled.

Click.

No response.

A rustle straight ahead caught his attention. "Rosane?"

A muffled cry was his answer. Stooping against the attic's low ceiling, he felt his way across the black space, ripped sticky nets of spiders, bumped his shoulder against a pile of boxes, banged his shin on the metal edge of a trunk. Slowly his eyes adjusted to the low streetlight scrimping past the dirty panes of the gabled window on his right. "Rosane?"

Fumée jumped at him, spitting and arching her back. The hair on her body stood on end and her eyes glowed a feral yellow. When Daniel reached out to her, she batted him with her paw, ears flattened and teeth bared, then flashed past him and bounded out the attic trapdoor.

Instinct more than a noise made him stand still. Something sliced the air to his left. He turned, holding his arm up protectively.

"Daniel, watch out!"

Rosane's warning came too late. The sturdy wooden goalie stick struck his forearm. A resounding crack filled the air. Pain shot up his arm, past his elbow and shinnied all the way up to his shoulder.

"Daniel!" Christiane's frightened cry came from below as her steps scrambled on the stairs.

"I'm all right. Stay down." He cradled his arm against his body. "Marguerite? *C'est Daniel.*"

"Daniel—" Rosane whimpered "—help me."

"Marguerite, come out here. Let's talk."

"No one care." Marguerite's gruff voice scraped like fingernails on slate against the darkness. "Give, give, give. Everyone want something from Marguerite. But who gives to me? No one. Now is my turn."

"Your turn for what?"

"To be happy."

Daniel's arm throbbed and the cuff of his dress shirt squeezed the skin around his wrist. Soft light suddenly filled the attic. A glance over his shoulder showed him the outline of Christiane's body in the stairwell as she placed a lantern on the floor. Body tense, he circled a stack of trunks. Two had been thrown from their perch, their contents strewn about the floor. What was Marguerite looking for? Carefully, he stepped over the pile of ancient clothes.

Marguerite cowered in the corner, holding Rosane by the waist with one arm, brandishing the goalie stick with the other. Cornered like a rat, she would fight. He had to gain her trust.

"Marguerite, can we talk?"

"Leave me alone." She squeezed Rosane tighter against her body. Rosane whimpered.

"Put the child down, Marguerite."

"She is mine!"

"Of course, but you don't want to hurt her, do you? Listen, she's crying. You take good care of the things you love."

Daniel fought his urge to charge Marguerite and rip Rosane from her clutches.

"I do." Marguerite sniffed. "I am a good mother."

"You know what I liked best about visiting your house when I was little? Your kitchen. It was nice and warm and always smelled so good."

"I am a good cook." A sad smile crinkled one side of Marguerite's mouth.

He kept his voice soft and soothing. "Any child would've been lucky to have you as a mother."

"He took my Amélie from me." Marguerite's eyes shone like wet pebbles.

"I know. That was wrong of Armand."

"I was sleeping, and he just take her." Pain kneaded Marguerite's face into grotesque folds.

"He had no right to do that."

"I love her."

"You have a big heart." Daniel kept his voice monotone, and advanced toward Marguerite with small steps.

"I didn't get to say goodbye."

"Christiane would like to say goodbye to Rosane."

Marguerite blinked at him and nodded, but didn't let go of the child.

"She loves her daughter, too."

Tears brimmed Marguerite's eyes. *"Ma petite…"*

"Your baby's all grown-up now. I'll help you find her."

"Armand, he know."

"We'll all help you find her," Daniel promised.

Marguerite stood unmoving, rocking her lost baby against her bosom.

"Rosane, come to me," Daniel urged, holding his right arm out to his daughter while keeping his gaze glued to Marguerite.

Rosane squirmed in Marguerite's grasp. Marguerite clamped Rosane to her breast like an old doll.

"Ma petite." Marguerite sniffed.

"Christiane's baby, Marguerite."

"Mon tour…"

"She's crying, Marguerite. Look at her face. Look how you're hurting her."

"Don't cry. *Grand-maman* will take care of you." Marguerite rocked Rosane back and forth against her chest.

"You're not her grandmother. She's not your grandchild."

"I love her."

"Rosane needs her mother."

"Daniel?" Christiane whispered. "Give her Amélie."

Something soft landed near his feet. Slowly he stooped to pick up the doll Marguerite had made for her lost infant. He crooked the rag doll in his arms as if it were a baby. "She's here, Marguerite. See, I have Amélie. She needs you."

"Amélie…" As if the goalie stick were too heavy for her to hold up, it drooped to Marguerite's side.

"She's here, Marguerite. Waiting for you."

He extended the doll just out of her reach. Marguerite's grip on Rosane loosened. Daniel rushed at Marguerite, pulled Rosane from Marguerite's hold and plunked the doll in her arms. Rosane clung tight to his waist, accepting his protective arm around her shoulder.

Daniel backed toward the stairs and nudged Rosane. "Go," he whispered. "Your mother is waiting for you."

The sound of sirens keened through the night.

Murmuring soft encouragement, he went toward Marguerite, who sobbed a fountain of tears as she rocked the doll against her heart. He plucked the hockey stick from her, then hugged her close. "It's all right. We'll take good care of you.'' Like a deflated balloon, Marguerite slumped against him, crushing his broken arm. Another victim of Armand's obsession.

Epilogue

The trip to the hospital and the two days that followed passed in a blur. Christi hadn't let Rosane out of her sight since the frightened child tumbled out of the black attic into her arms. She'd let Daniel handle everything from the police to the media to having Marguerite transferred to a long-term psychiatric clinic. Though he took care of her and Rosane's every need, it was as if the mere sight of them caused him pain. His eyes were blank slates. His stiff politeness nauseating.

She fanned her return tickets in her hand. The plane was scheduled to take off at two-thirty. She didn't have much time to get herself together. And she certainly didn't want to analyze the regret sighing through her limbs like an unfulfilled desire.

He didn't want them. Even after she'd forgiven him for his cruel playacting with Armand. He'd been trying to do what he'd done for nine years—keep her and Rosane safe.

Rosane and Fumée played happily on the floor of Daniel's guest room at her feet.

"Do you have everything packed?" Christi asked.

"Will I be able to say goodbye to Isabelle?" Fumée rolled to have her tummy scratched.

"We'll make sure you do." Christi jammed the tickets in her purse.

"How will I take Fumée home with me? We don't have one of those cages."

"Oh, honey, Fumée can't come with us right now. She doesn't have her papers from the vet. Daniel will take good care of her. We'll get you another kitten when we get home."

Rosane hugged the kitten to her chest and threw Christi daggers of rebellion. "No! I want Fumée."

"I'm sorry. I know Fumée means a lot to you. But they won't let her across the border without some special papers. How about if Daniel takes her to the vet, then ships her to us?"

Rosane shrugged one shoulder, then gave a slow nod.

"Why don't you help me pack?"

She'd thought that Armand's death would free her from fear and confusion. That somehow the stable roots she'd come to find two weeks ago would magically appear. But no, nothing had come except this nagging vacuum that sucked what little energy she had left into some dark hole. She hadn't gone back to Armand's house. The answers weren't there.

Returning to Texas and putting some kind of life back together was the best thing to do. The safe thing. The logical thing. It wasn't as if Daniel had asked them to stay. His cold demeanor seemed to scream that he couldn't wait to have them out of his life. There was no reason for marriage, he'd told her. She was safe. She didn't need his protection.

Only his love. That was the one thing he couldn't give her.

She stuffed the last of her belongings into the suitcase, zipped the sides and locked the clasp. There was only one thing left to do—let Daniel know they were ready to leave.

She found Daniel on the phone in his studio. He motioned her to sit. Her choices were the piano bench where Daniel had started his seduction or the leather couch where they'd made love. She sat on the bottom stair and waited.

"I just wanted to let you know the taxi should be here in twenty minutes," she said when he put the phone down.

"I'll drive you."

"That's all right. I don't want to impose." *Ask me to stay. Please ask us to stay. I don't need to hear you love me, just that you need us.*

"I'll drive you."

Stomach sinking, she nodded toward his cast. "Your arm."

"It's the left. I can still shift."

His voice was stripped of all color, as dead as the cold knot lodged inside her chest. Christi nodded and motioned stiffly toward the stairs. "I'll bring down our bags."

"Christiane?"

She glanced at him over her shoulder. As much as she'd wanted words from him, she didn't want to hear what his eyes foretold.

"It's for the best. For you. For Rosane."

His words were smoke. They had no substance. She'd been wrong to hope so long for them.

Tears rattling like loose change in her chest, she ran up the stairs, leaving the remaining pieces of her heart behind.

LETTING CHRISTIANE and Rosane go was the hardest thing he'd ever done. He couldn't face his empty home. He'd see traces of Christiane everywhere, smell her perfume, hear her voice.

The picture Rosane had drawn for him would stare at him from the refrigerator door. There would be no girlish giggles, no tumble of girl and kitten slip sliding through his house, no piles of girl-size shoes, sweaters and storybooks to stumble over.

"You'll write to me, won't you?" Rosane had whispered to him as he'd hugged her at the airport. He'd nodded, his throat too tight to answer.

He found himself driving on Boulevard Champlain toward his mother's gallery. The warm atmosphere at Le Petit Coin enveloped him as soon as he walked in. His mother's bear hug offered him a measure of comfort.

"How are you?" his mother asked, concern crinkling the corners of her eyes.

"They just left."

His mother hugged him again and led him toward her office. He flopped into the nearest chair. She poured him a cup of coffee. "Did you ask her to stay?"

"No."

"Well, why not?"

She was angry now. Chantal had accepted the role of grandmother with zeal after the theater incident and had spent long hours trying to catch up on the years she'd missed with Rosane. Now she saw his selfishness as cheating her out of a grandchild. She couldn't understand that he'd let them go because he'd already taken too much from them. "Papa."

"What?" She pounded her cup onto the desktop and propped her hands on her hips, leaning toward him, disappointment seeping from every line of her body, like the time she'd caught him stealing bubblegum from the corner convenience store when he was nine. "You are nothing like your father."

"You don't know the things I've done." He squirmed under his mother's all-knowing gaze.

"Yes, I do." Her gaze softened. She crouched beside him and took his hands in hers. "You can love. Your father never could."

"Why did you marry him then?"

Chantal rose and moved to stare out the small window. "He was a handsome, charming man. I loved him. I thought I could change him. I thought my love was enough for both of us. But you can't change people." Regret at a lesson learned too late hitched her shoulders. "You haven't tried to change Christiane and that precious daughter of yours. And she hasn't tried to change you. You love each other as you are."

"But love…" Daniel lifted his shoulders helplessly. "It kept you prisoner. I don't want—"

"They love you. That is everything."

The phone rang. Chantal cocked her head toward the sound. "I've been waiting for a call from Vancouver. I'll take it in the shop. Stay as long as you like."

Daniel left the shop, but didn't climb into his car. He kept walking and ended up at the ferry dock. The icy wind whipped his hair and chapped his cheeks. The sky was the same gray as Christiane's eyes. He leaned on the metal fence and watched aimlessly as the ferry rammed itself through the river's ice.

He loved Christiane. And he loved Rosane. Life without them would be an empty hole.

He slid his father's ring from his finger and stared at the black star sapphire stone. "I forgive you, Papa. Your mistakes aren't mine. I won't let the people I love slip away from me the way you did."

He hurled the ring into the St. Lawrence and watched it disappear between two chunks of ice.

"Mom?" Rosane asked as they waited for their connection in Chicago.

"Mmm." The original one-hour mechanical delay had stretched into three.

"I read Daniel's letter." Rosane's fuchsia jacket hung open. Her book lay carelessly splattered at her feet.

"And?"

"He wanted me."

Christi wrapped an arm around her daughter's shoulders and hugged her close. "Of course he did."

"Do you love him?" Rosane zipped the zipper slide up and down one side of the jacket.

Christi stared out at the blue taxi lights on the airport apron. "I always will."

"Then why did we leave? Why can't we be a family?"

"Because…" Christi sighed and shook her head. "Because being a grown-up is complicated sometimes."

"He loves you, you know."

"In his own way." She hunched her shoulders and sank more deeply into the stiff lounge chair.

"But Mom, you either do or you don't. That's what's important. The doing part."

Christi tweaked Rosane's nose. "When did you get so smart?"

Rosane dropped her head on Christi's shoulder. "Will we ever see him again?"

"I don't know." How often could she hand him her heart only to have him reject it?

Rosane kicked at the lounge chair with the heel of her boot. "When are we going to get home?"

"Soon, I hope. They'll call us when the plane is ready."

"I'm hungry."

"Okay, let's go find a snack," Christi said, glad enough for the diversion. Rosane's questions opened up feelings she would rather keep bottled until she safely released them in the privacy of her own home. "What do you feel like eating?"

"Ice cream!"

"Ice cream? Brrr! It's freezing."

Hand stuffed into Christi's, Rosane bounced along at her side. "Chocolate, double-scoop."

"How about—" She stopped midsentence when, through the sea of milling passengers, she thought she saw Daniel. Could anyone else have eyes that brandy color? She shook her head and plowed on. A trick of the light, that was all.

"Mom? Look, it's Daniel!" Rosane launched herself into Daniel's arms. A big smile creasing his face, he caught his daughter with his right arm and held the casted one out of harm's way. He looked as if the weight of the world had somehow been lifted from his shoulders.

Before she could find her voice, Daniel spoke. "I

love you, Christiane. I don't want you to go back to Fort Worth. Stay with me." His words rushed out, as sweet a melody as she'd ever heard. "Or let me come stay with you. It doesn't matter. I want to make up for all I've missed." He hugged his daughter close. "I want to see my little girl grow up. I want the good, the bad. I want...everything. I need both of you."

The last word came out as an anguished whisper and Christi barely heard it above the noise of the crowded terminal.

A chain reaction of emotion tumbled through her like popcorn under heat. He loved her. He wanted her. He needed her.

"Marry me, Christiane."

Joy leapt through her, swelled her heart and could have lit up a small country. "I'll have all of you, too. Even the silence, Daniel. As long as you're here."

"Does that mean we're a family now?" Rosane asked, her gaze bouncing from her mother's tear-streaked face to her father's goofy grin.

"It sure does." Christi reached up to Daniel's neck and brought his head down to meet her kiss. She was finally home.

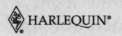

Like a phantom in the night
comes an exciting promotion from

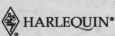
HARLEQUIN®

INTRIGUE®

GOTHIC ROMANCE

Look for a provocative
gothic-themed thriller each month
by your favorite Intrigue authors!
Once you surrender to the classic
blend of chilling suspense and
electrifying romance in these
gripping page-turners, there will
be no turning back....

Available wherever Harlequin books are sold.

HARLEQUIN®
Live the emotion™

www.eHarlequin.com

HIE3

SPOTLIGHT

**"Debra Webb's fast-paced thriller will make you
shiver in passion and fear...."**—*Romantic Times*

Dying To Play

Debra Webb

When FBI agent Trace Callahan
arrives in Atlanta to investigate
a baffling series of multiple
homicides, deputy chief of
detectives Elaine Jentzen isn't
prepared for the immediate
attraction between them. And as
they hunt to find the killer known
as the Gamekeeper, it seems that
Trace is singled out as his next
victim...unless Elaine can stop the
Gamekeeper before it's too late.

Available January 2005.

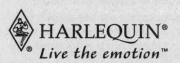
Live the emotion™

**Exclusive
Bonus Features:**
Author Interview
Sneak Preview...
and more!

www.eHarlequin.com   PHDTP

If you enjoyed what you just read,
then we've got an offer you can't resist!

Take 2 bestselling love stories FREE!

Plus get a FREE surprise gift!

Clip this page and mail it to Harlequin Reader Service®

IN U.S.A.
3010 Walden Ave.
P.O. Box 1867
Buffalo, N.Y. 14240-1867

IN CANADA
P.O. Box 609
Fort Erie, Ontario
L2A 5X3

YES! Please send me 2 free Harlequin Intrigue® novels and my free surprise gift. After receiving them, if I don't wish to receive anymore, I can return the shipping statement marked cancel. If I don't cancel, I will receive 4 brand-new novels each month, before they're available in stores! In the U.S.A., bill me at the bargain price of $4.24 plus 25¢ shipping and handling per book and applicable sales tax, if any*. In Canada, bill me at the bargain price of $4.99 plus 25¢ shipping and handling per book and applicable taxes**. That's the complete price and a savings of at least 10% off the cover prices—what a great deal! I understand that accepting the 2 free books and gift places me under no obligation ever to buy any books. I can always return a shipment and cancel at any time. Even if I never buy another book from Harlequin, the 2 free books and gift are mine to keep forever.

181 HDN DZ7N
381 HDN DZ7P

Name _____ (PLEASE PRINT)

Address _____ Apt.#

City _____ State/Prov. _____ Zip/Postal Code

Not valid to current Harlequin Intrigue® subscribers.

Want to try two free books from another series?
Call 1-800-873-8635 or visit www.morefreebooks.com.

* Terms and prices subject to change without notice. Sales tax applicable in N.Y.
** Canadian residents will be charged applicable provincial taxes and GST.
   All orders subject to approval. Offer limited to one per household.
   ® are registered trademarks owned and used by the trademark owner and or its licensee.

INT04R   ©2004 Harlequin Enterprises Limited